Willbom

Moon & the Grave Digger

Moon & the Grave Digger

William E. Thedford

Tate Publishing & *Enterprises*

Moon and the Grave Digger

Published by Tate Publishing & Enterprises, LLC
127 E. Trade Center Terrace | Mustang, Oklahoma 73064 USA
1.888.361.9473 | www.tatepublishing.com

Tate Publishing is committed to excellence in the publishing industry. The company reflects the philosophy established by the founders, based on Psalm 68:11,
"The Lord gave the word and great was the company of those who published it."

Cover design by Tyler Evans
Interior design by Stephanie Woloszyn

Published in the United States of America

ISBN: 978-1-61663-165-9
1. Fiction / Mystery & Detective / General
10.05.14

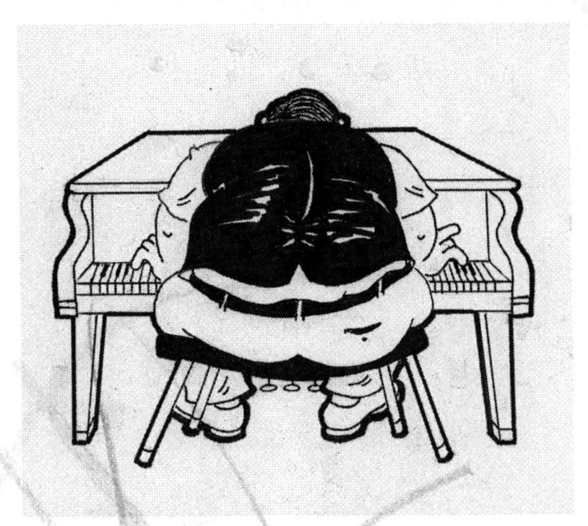

Dedication

This book is dedicated to my loving wife, Brenda Coleman Thedford, for her Christian guidance, support, and love. For her long hours of work refining my script, but most of all, the laughs and enjoyment as she and I worked together.

Acknowledgment

To Miss Tammy Wood, a wagon load of thank you for her timely assistance through proofing and technical assistance from the start to finish of the my manuscript. A true Christian friend.

To Mr. Buddy Leuty, a high school classmate that shared the memories of Springo. Sketches from his pen provided a needed connection from reality to fiction.

Table of Contents

Preface

They were characters of a time once lived in a place that can never return as it once was. Their impact on family, friends, and community lives on in other places, both far and near.

Oh, to return to the days of youth, this can never occur, except by our pleasures of mind enhanced by the fiction herein.

In the Beginning

It was a typically hot August day at Moon Milligan's gas station located on the corner of Highway 27 and Piccadilly Avenue in Springo. A hot weather haze had settled between the mountain and the small East Tennessee town. The only visible work going on downtown was the two red lights on Highway 27 and the one over by the post office on Front Street.

Moon, all six foot two inches and three hundred and ten pounds, was delicately balanced on the back legs of his cane-bottomed chair against the cigarette machine. Sweat rolled off his forehead and down his face, crossing his double row of sweat beads. The mixture of sweat and the dust from the station had accumulated in the folds of the big man's neck.

The hum of the window air conditioner had decreased the view from Moon's eyes to small slits that drew increasingly smaller by the minute. *Bam,* the door from the bay of the station flew all the way open and slammed against the trash can next to Moon. The eye slits increased to half open.

"What's up, Lesiel?" Moon inquired.

"That tar won't go on the rim. Hubert even greased it good, still won't go on!" Lesiel explained.

Moon leaned slightly forward and gravity brought the front chair legs abruptly to the floor. As he followed Lesiel out into the bay, there was Hubert, wet with sweat from head to toe.

"Hot, ain't it, Moon?" Hubert mumbled.

"Hot, Hubert. Try that fifteen-inch tire I leaned up next to the changer. It'll work better than this fourteen. Don't grease it either," Moon ordered as he turned and walked away.

"Told you that was the wrong tar," Lesiel said.

"Both got white walls," Hubert insisted.

Brothers, Hubert and Lesiel didn't ride into town on a wagonload of pumpkins. They were pulling the wagon! Lesiel was tall with a body as if chiseled from steel, and Hubert was shorter with bulging muscles; however, their strength stopped at their shoulders. Hubert was the leader, of sorts. After all, he made it all the way to the second six-week period of his freshman year at Springo High. Lesiel took a U-turn between the seventh and eighth grades.

Now Moon was another story. He was highly intelligent, talented—that's with a capital T—and musically gifted. He could play a piano.

He started playing publicly at the age of fourteen. A young man by the name of Mitchell, of legal age, would take him to Rockwood to a beer joint called The Junction, or most called it Floyd Daughty's Place. Moon would play well into the night and early Sunday hours for pocket change and a few beers. Afterward, he would be dropped off across the street from Springo First

Methodist Church in time for Sunday school, waiting across the street for his friend Bill to come to church with his mother. Moon would hurry across the street, always speaking first to Bill's mom, then whispering in Bill's ear, "I spent the night at your house!"

It was several years later before Bill found out where Moon had been on those Saturday nights. It was hard to believe the two mothers never got together, as both were in the same Sunday school class.

Moon had married Betty Jo Griffin four years after graduating from Springo High. He was working for the State of Tennessee Highway Department. He was supervisor of a road crew.

Betty Jo came from the other side of the Tennessee River; she was born and raised in Meigs County.

Moon would introduce her as an orphan he had picked up in Mages County. This would rile the little lady. Truth was, she came from a farming family. She grew up with three brothers and two sisters.

Mrs. Griffin, Betty Jo's mother, loved for Moon to come a courting, as she put it, 'cause she loved to watch that boy eat.

Mr. Randolph Griffin had a totally different take on the situation.

"Boy, you ain't gonna make no money playing that music, and as soon as they get that sorry democrat governor out of there, you won't have a job either!" he would rant.

"Now, Randy!" Moon would say. Just calling him Randy would ruffle his feathers even more. "There will always be a democrat in the governor's mansion, a republican would be too tight to buy paint, and the mansion would rot down," the big guy joked and tried to pat him on the back, but Randolph would stomp out of the room.

Betty Jo, or Jo, as Moon called her most of the time, was a pleasant, easygoing, pretty young thing. When asked how he was able to make such a catch, Moon would firmly state, "She's from Mage's County and her daddy paid me a lot of money to take her across the river and never bring her back!"

"He gave you money if *you* promised to never come back! He sends me money every month to leave you!" she would fire back.

She was the perfect fit for the big, moody guy. Betty Jo had a calming effect on Moon. She was always the one to lift his spirits. As he played the piano at gigs, she would always stand behind him, mostly in the background, but only a step away if he was in need of anything.

Moon treated his Jo as if she were a fragile piece of fine China. His father-in-law was right about one thing, though, a republican governor was elected, but Moon's departure from the highway job had nothing to do with politics. He left because of hot asphalt on ninety-degree days and twenty mile per hour winds on twenty-nine degree days.

H.R. Milligan, Moon's father, lent Moon the money to buy the Shell Station. It had a good trade. The owner wanted to retire and get off his feet. Moon strengthened the relationships with the customers he liked, and the rest... well, they moved up or down Highway 27 to find a station they were more compatible with.

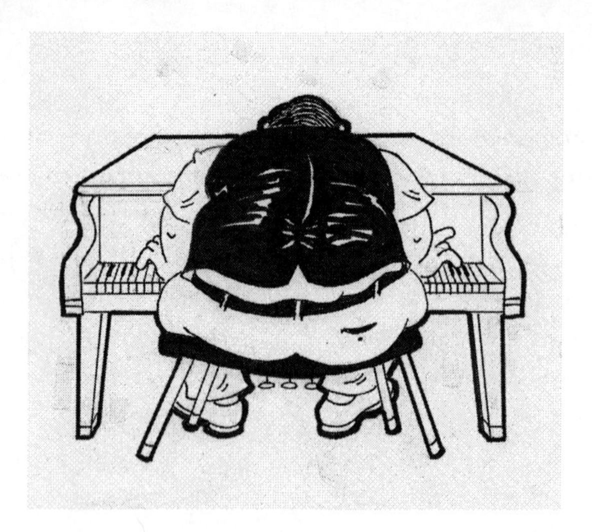

Europe Bound

Springo had a famous musician, a blind piano player, Hargis Robbins, known professionally as Pig Robbins in Nashville. Hargis won Instrumentalist of the Year twice at the Grand Ole Opry. He was a regular for Dolly Parton and received credit on many of her earlier recordings.

Hargis was blinded at the age of three and was sent to the Tennessee's school for the blind. There he learned the keys to the piano as one of the early exercises for blind children. It became quickly evident that he had special talent. Hargis didn't learn piano, he just started playing and quickly mastered it.

Pig would say that the keyboard never changes; light or dark, old or new, it's always the same, only the players change.

Pig was going on tour to Europe with several of the Opry stars of the time. He made a special trip to Springo as soon as the trip became a reality. His brother, Billy Ray, drove Hargis out to Moon's house. Billy Ray had been a chauffeur for the Opry star for several years. Moon and

Betty Jo were always happy to see their friend, and Moon immediately asked if Hargis had a new number to show him.

"I came on business, Moon! Got a gig, thought you would be interested in. You and I could do our dueling bit like we've done here in this room many times. Good money! I'll see—*ha, ha, ha*—make sure that you get taken care of," the blind man stated. "We'd be playing before sold out crowds and see new places." Hargis paused.

"Wait a minute. See new places? You know I only want one-nighters! I don't care to stray far from Springo, but if you're talking about New York or the west coast . . . just forget it," Moon firmly spoke.

"This is special, Moon, you will never forget the—"

"Where?" Moon interrupts.

"Europe. England, France, Italy, Germany," Hargis stated.

"You've got to be kidding me! What's the punchline?" Moon inquired.

"Money, Moon! More than you've ever taken in before and all expenses paid. You won't have to pay a cent for anything. The best part, you will have a feature performance at every stop. We will do the duel and get equal billing. We fly over in ten days!" Hargis concluded.

Moon got quiet, then a grin spread across his face. "Wow!" Then he went silent again. After a moment, Moon said firmly to Hargis, "Betty Jo goes, if I go!"

"Moon, that's not going to be possible; everything has been set. It'll be you and me, and Billy Ray will go to assist me," Hargis explained.

"Betty Jo goes if I go!" Moon demanded.

"Moon, that's not going to happen. I've already been

there with the promoters; they gave me one extra slot for you specially, and that's it!" Hargis said.

"I'm not going," the big boy firmly stated.

"Yes, you are, Moon Milligan!" Betty Jo interjected.

"No!" Moon answered.

Out of character for Betty Jo, her temple wrinkled as she stared straight at her husband. With her fist, she slammed the table, sending a half-full cup of coffee, with the matching saucer, cascading onto the floor with a crash. Two grown men, their eyes the size of saucers, and the third man, dropping his walking stick, were stricken with a silent lack of movement.

As they boarded the plane in New York for their flight to Frankfurt, Moon playfully asked the flight attendant if he needed two tickets.

"Only if you decide to come back," she answered with a smile.

Some of the performers were allowed to take their instruments onboard the plane, but the bass guitars and drums had to be checked in. The artists were constantly worrying about their instruments. Pig and Moon kept the attendants wondering about their claim of bringing their personal pianos onboard with them. They told them to listen closely at landing for the sound of the keys if it was a rough landing. Pig told them to let him know if his piano was off key. He would point to his dark glasses and cane and then say he could not tell if he was off key.

The overnight flight to Frankfurt was terrible. Moon

could not get comfortable in the two-seat arrangement they had made for the big man. Teasing, Moon told the attendants that he was Little Richard's brother and that they had come from a mixed marriage. One of the girls was amazed. She said she didn't know that that was possible, but it didn't matter to her.

Upon arrival at Frankfurt Airport, it was discovered that Moon's luggage had been lost. It was decided that the airline would deliver the luggage to the hotel when it was found. By the time they reached their rooms, Moon got a call to come to the lobby. As he approached the front desk, he saw Crain, the tour manager, standing with a worried look on his face.

"Mr. Milligan, the airline called and said your luggage was put on the wrong plane. We're trying to find a tailor to fit you a suit to match Pig's, like the one we made for you in Nashville. The sequined design is a big problem here," he concluded.

Moon was surprised when, within minutes, two gentlemen from the hotel staff had he and Mr. Crain, along with Pig's suit, in a taxi and on their way to a tailor.

The little, short tailor put his hands on his head as he saw the size of the big American. He started jabbering in German to the two ladies that were assisting him.

Moon had a blue dress shirt on that he had purchased in the states. It was a good fit, and the little man requested that Moon take it off and leave it. He said he would have the suit ready by show time.

Moon was quite a sight as he left the tailor's shop and arrived back at the busy hotel. As usual, his sport coat was held in place with one overstressed button. Under the coat, his T-shirt did not cover the bottom six inches of his belly skin. Moon didn't mind; he was ready for a nap. He had chosen not to go on a sightseeing tour of the medieval Romerplatz and cathedral that had been spared from the destruction of the 1944 bombings. He decided that, due to wardrobe problems and the need for shuteye, he would decline. Pig had opted out of the sightseeing tour too, but being good-natured, he requested any tour given to him be in black and white, no color ... please.

Pig's piano was set on stage, as he was the featured pianist, and Moon's was set on rollers. Typically, as they would start the duel, Moon would play a few notes of classical music and Pig would drown him out with country rock and roll. This would continue until they joined on the country side to a standing ovation. They would switch roles throughout the tour.

From Frankfurt to Rothenburg to Munich, and the mountain-ringed Innsbruck in Austria, the routine was the same; perform, hotel, bus ride; perform, hotel, bus ride.

One thing remained the same, shuffling the cards. As the bus rolled on through the countryside, Moon would play cards for hours. The late nights flew into early morning hours and from bus to hotel to bus again. As the flow of booze would take its toll, ol' Springo would outlast the Nashville boys, night after night. A scenic drive took them to Brenner Pass, the Italian border, and onto the Dolomite Mountains, before reaching the unique, canal-crossed city of Venice.

The card playing stopped for Moon. He was on orders from Betty Jo to take a roll of pictures. On orders from Springo, he started snapping shots as they traveled by private launch along a series of canals with Palladian architecture on each side. By the time he reached St. Mark's Square, the little camera had snapped two and a half rolls of film. Moon loaded the camera again as he toured St. Mark's Basilica and was ready for the main event—to take a ride in a less-than-romantic gondola. He wasn't too excited about the adventure, but that was soon to change. As he paid and prepared to step aboard the narrow, tipsy, little boat, Moon wondered if Betty Jo realized the ends he would go through to please her.

As the first step was taken, everything seemed to shift into slow motion. The gondolier realized Moon was standing too close to the front. The gondola next to Moon's boat was filled with musicians that saw disaster in the making. The gondola on the other side had just docked and was occupied by two young couples, and the gondolier, who likewise sensed the impending disaster. *Action:* Moon's weight in the forward motion had irreversibly committed him to the first downward step:

(1) The host gondola was flipped up in the air.

(2) Moon had lost his balance and was shifting critically to the right.

(3) His camera had been launched in the opposite direction as he threw his arm out in an attempt to regain his balance.

Solution:

(A) The gondolier in the couples' gondola and the trumpet player in the musicians' gondola grabbed Moon's gondola and kept him from de-boarding.

(B) Another couple in the couples' gondola and a flute player and a violinist in the musicians' boat grabbed Moon by each arm and lowered him into his seat.

(C) The girl from the second couple in the couples' gondola caught the camera. And, oh yes, her boyfriend hunkered down in the bottom of the boat in a fetal position. He was said to be French.

Speaking of the French, Moon was looking forward to Paris. The group would be guests at Paris's most famous cabaret, Le Moulin Rouge dinner and show. The next morning, they would visit the Eiffel Tower and take a riverboat on the Seine and then board a ferry at Calais to the White Cliffs of Dover. They had one more show in London. Moon had been battling a bug and was beginning to get homesick for his beloved Springo.

As Moon returned home, he told one and all, "I'll never leave Springo again, except for a one-nighter."

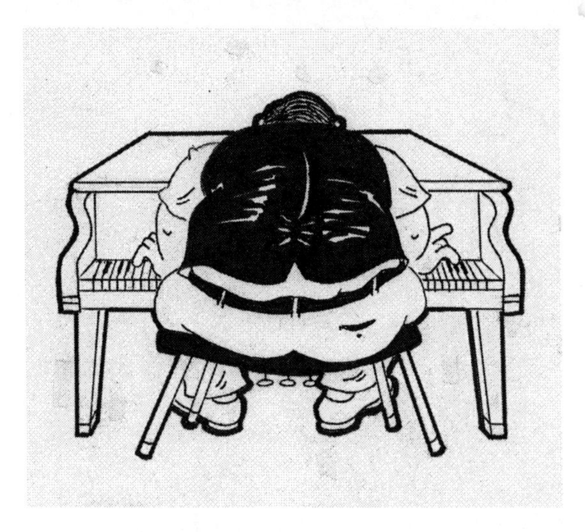

The Station

One of Moon's hidden talents was solving crime stories at movies or on TV. Before the detectives had it figured out, Moon would tell everyone in hearing distance the outcome.

His wife, Betty Jo, wasn't a big fan of his when it came to solving the crime halfway through the film. Now, solving the crime was only half the fun. Next came trying to find out a way to turn it into the perfect crime.

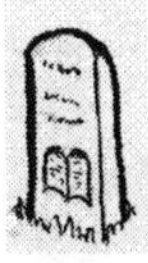

Today, the heat and the presence of Hubert and Lesiel taxed Moon's ability to enjoy his adventures of the mind. One thing worse than the heat—Granny, Hubert, and Lesiel's grandmother.

"Oh, please, Lord, give me a customer—gas, fan belt, grease job," Moon prayed. "Too late to hide!"

"Hi, Moon. What's them boys doin'?" Granny asked as she stood with the door open.

"They are drinkin,' playin' poker, and drinkin'!" Moon teased. "Now close the door, you're letting all the cool out."

"Ohooo, if for a minute, I believed my boys would do anything like that. I would box their ears and their poor departed Daddy Frank would rise from his grave and haunt them the rest of their years. God bless him and rest his soul!" Granny wailed.

"Granny, Hubert's twenty-four and Lesiel must be twenty-one," Moon said.

"I promised Daddy Frank I'd raise them boys straight and true, God bless him and rest his soul."

Daddy Frank, the boys' father, had left for Atlanta when he was a young man. He married the boys' mother, and when Hubert was six and Lesiel three, she ran off with a man from Texas. Frank loaded the boys up in his pick-up, headed back to Springo, and moved in with his widowed mother.

The boys called her Granny and their father Daddy Frank. It stuck, and the pair became known to all as Granny and Daddy Frank.

Two years after his return to Tennessee, Frank was driving a loaded log truck down Grandview Mountain when the left front tire blew out. According to the eye-witnesses in the car behind him, the truck crossed the highway, slammed into the guardrail, veered back across the road, and hit the rock bluff. The load broke loose and crushed Frank. Churches and the good folk raised money for a proper burial and had enough money left over to give to Granny and the boys. Granny vowed to raise the boys true and straight in honor of Daddy Frank. Church was mandatory for them, though it became obvious that they were not developing in their scholastic skills. Granny was overprotective at every turn in their lives, and they were very dependent on her!

Granny and the boys lived across Piney Creek away from the metropolis area of Springo's population of 2,047. Sandtown Road ran from Highway 68 along the creek down to Highway 27. Her small two-bedroom home, while dated, was as neat as a pin. It had green shutters and sidewalks that Hubert and Lesiel had lain from the brick that came from the demolition of Springo's only hotel of days gone by. Granny also owned a small strip of land, about an acre and a half, across the road on the banks of Piney. Her late husband, Arnold, had built a small barn on it and at one time kept a milk cow and several goats. The boys had played in the barn and along the creek. Nowadays, the barn was in ill repair with part of the roof missing and the whole thing leaning toward the creek.

Hubert had promised that he and his brother would fix it up when they got around to it (round-to-its were hard to come by for the boys).

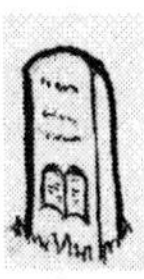

Moon's attention shifted from Granny to the front of the station as the dinger went off by the pumps. It was Johnson's Furniture Store's delivery truck.

"Lesiel get the front," Moon bellowed as he had

calculated the stress of the day's heat compared with listening to Granny. She won. The heat was too much!

Moon and Granny had an agreement about the boys. They would hang around the station and help and run errands when needed. They would not be on the payroll and would be paid cash for their efforts. Moon would act as their unofficial agent in securing part-time work from townsfolk and make sure they were paid and treated fairly. Many days, Moon would pay them a few dollars, even if he had nothing for them to do. He was good to them but at times enjoyed laughs at their expense.

Certain customers preferred that the pair didn't pump their gas or check under the hood, so Moon was selective in sending them out. Most townsfolk enjoyed the pair, as they were always upbeat and wore smiles each time they were there. While they did not make sound decisions relating to their tasks, they followed instructions and always tried to please.

Hubert rushed back into the station, "Moon, Jerry said Mr. E.W. wanted me and Lesiel to go help unload all that stuff off the truck. Its got washers, stoves, beds, and couches on it! They got to take it all the way out the other side of Wolfcreek on Watts Bar Lake! We got their old stuff to pick up too!" excitedly he spewed out.

"Go ahead, I'll make it here," Moon replied.

Granny opened the door and hollered out, "Jerry! Jerry, you drive careful and don't drive too fast."

"Yes, 'em, Miss Granny. We'll be back in a while," Jerry answered.

Granny turned back to Moon and was excited that the boys had some work. She started talking a mile a minute. *Ring, ring. Saved by the bell,* Moon thought.

"Moon. Ray here. A fellow just stopped by here selling forty-gallon galvanized trash cans. They're seconds. They have sharp edges around the top where the weld doesn't match, but commercial grade, heavy duty cans. A shop grinder will take care of the edges in a jiffy. I'm getting eight of them. He has four more. They're five bucks a can if you want 'em. I'll go ahead and pay for 'em," Ray explained.

"Yea, I'll take 'em. I'll send the money over with Hubert and Lesiel when they get back, thanks," Moon responded as he pulled a clean shop rag from a box and wiped his face.

Paul and Ray Lyons ran the Gulf station across the street from Moon, and while they sold gas, their main thrust was auto parts with a garage in the rear. They got along well with Moon, but it was not so for Moon and some of the other local station owners. Moon, at times, was very moody, and if you didn't know him well, his moods could sour you for life. For those that knew him well, he was just a big, really big, kid at times, but he would do anything for you if you were in need.

Ray hung up the phone, but Moon continued holding the phone to his ear and occasionally mumbling into it.

Oh, a customer at last, Moon thought. He stepped past Granny, and before she could say a word, in a loud voice he greeted the special customer.

"George, how you doin? See the little woman let you out of the house," Moon said.

"Joyce left me, man, didn't—*sniff, sniff*—you know? Kids and all," George dead panned.

"Oh, man. I didn't know. I'm sorry. Gee, when did it happen?" Moon whispered.

"Got you, big guy! *Ha, ha, ha.* Got you good," George gloated.

"Gas will cost you two dollars a gallon. You sucked me in. I was about to cry, 'cause Joyce told me she would run off with me!" Moon responded with a shot of his own.

"Moon, I got to get home. Tell Hubert to drive careful. That ol' truck of his needs tires," Granny said as she moved next to the men.

"That ol' truck's got good tires on it. I gave them the set!" Moon reminded Granny.

"Used tires, it has got used tires," Granny replied.

"Got used tires on my Jeep, Granny. People trade tires just because they want white walls, nothing wrong with their tires!" Moon snapped back, somewhat annoyed.

"Said the tires on that log truck Daddy Frank was a drivin' was good. He's dead, God bless him and rest his soul," Granny said as she walked off.

Moon looked at George as the smiles disappeared. They weren't in a joking mood any longer.

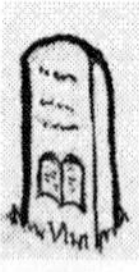

As Moon stepped back into the office, there stood Lloyd.

"Lloyd, you slipped in while I was talking to George. What you been doing?" Moon inquired.

"Mowin' over at the cemetery. 'Bout too hot to be standing under a shade tree, let alone mowin.' That air conditioner's just a fannin' today. Why don't you get you a new one, something bigger. That thing hasn't worked right since you got it," Lloyd let off steam.

"I traded some sorry gravedigger a real good refrigerator for it," Moon shot back.

Lloyd, the gravedigger, as he was known around Springo, loved to trade guns, knives, coins . . . it didn't matter. A sharp mind and a memory second to none, a hard worker, he had worked for Vaughn's Funeral Home for most of his adult life. He could tell you where anyone's grave lay and what type headstone it had. He mowed, trimmed, and planted flowers a lot of the time on his day off or in the evening.

A backhoe had been used for years to dig the graves, but Lloyd was always there to lay out the site. When the backhoe finished and moved away, Lloyd would climb down into the grave to clean out the corners and level the bottom.

If you were walking around the cemetery and happened to walk by the unfinished grave, it was startling for a shovel of dirt to come flying out. If Lloyd caught a glimpse of a flower delivery truck coming to the cemetery for an early delivery, he would jump back into the grave. As he silently crouched in the corner, he would listen as someone neared the site. A low groan would waft from the pit, and more times than not, the flowers would not make it all the way to the site.

Once, after waiting for the sound of the van's motor to shut off, Lloyd crept up his four-step ladder and peered out of the grave. The delivery boy was sitting in the truck trying to figure out why the wreaths and stands of flowers were strewed about. The flowers were laying fifteen feet from the grave. Slipping back into the grave, Lloyd placed his hands over his head and extended his arms upward and crept back up the ladder. As he reached the top of the grave, he let out a loud moan, followed by a hideous laugh. He could hear the sounds of the revving engine and gravel flying as the van fishtailed down the road.

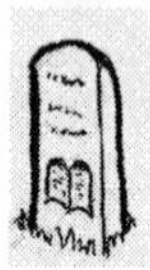

Hubert and Lesiel got out of Johnson's delivery truck and walked toward the door as Bear Harrison disappeared around the corner, heading to his garage.

"Moon, Hubert let his side slip, and we dropped the refrigerator on the front walk and broke off a piece of the concrete," Lesiel excitedly told.

Hubert insisted, "Not so! You let your side—"

"Shut up about the sidewalk. What did it do to the refrigerator?" Moon angrily inquired.

"Busted it pretty bad, bent the door until it won't close," Lesiel replied.

"Boys, that cost you more than you'll make in a month," Moon snapped.

"Na ah, hit was the old icebox," Lesiel explained.

"Boys, Granny said for you to drive careful and go straight home. See you tomorrow," Moon ended.

"See you," Hubert and Lesiel answered in unison.

Moon was glad that the day was winding down.

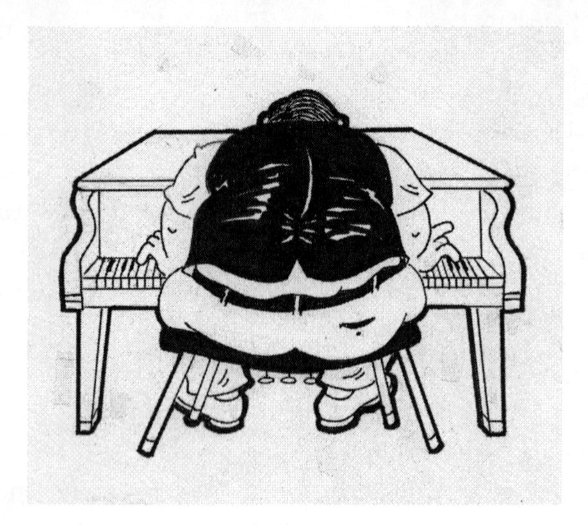

Mattie

Lloyd lived on Sandtown Road, about a quarter mile from Granny's place and across the road from the creek and Mattie Brown's house.

Mattie was a black... no, now as she would defiantly say, "Call me colored, call me Negro, but honey, I'm no more black than you are white," and then she would follow up with, "I'm just Aunt Jemima with a makeover," as she playfully flipped her hair and wiggled her hips. This would melt any animosity quicker than a hailstorm on an asphalt road in July.

Mattie had traveled a long, hard road to end up in Springo. Her great, great grandfather was a slave on the mega Buckhead Plantation, south of Atlanta. At fifteen, Mattie's great grandmother ran off with a young slave from a neighboring plantation. It was just prior to the start of the Civil War.

R.B. Buckhead owned several hundred acres, his three sons and Mattie's great, great grandfather, George, ran the plantation. R.B. was not liked by many of his fellow plantation owners because of the special privileges he gave his slaves. He built a small school, and his wife and daughters taught the plantation children until the age of twelve. Most all learned to read and write.

What infuriated his neighbors was his fall festival. All work stopped for four days. Hogs were lined up on spits for cooking over hickory. The women were in groups peeling potatoes, shelling field peas, picking, and cooking okra. The mansion's kitchen smelled like a pie factory.

What really ticked off the landlord's of the neighboring plantations was the open invitation to any and all slaves to come join in on Saturday and Sunday. Many owners forbid their slaves from attending, and this led to many problems for their plantations later.

It was at one of these celebrations that the fifteen-year-old girl ran off. George was furious that his daughter, Cece, had gone with Boomer from the Bowden Plantation.

Mr. Buckhead said that this "no good boy from ol' man Bowden's place had stole one of his girls." He was outraged. Word got out that the Buckhead people were coming after Boomer, and he and Cece took off in the middle of the night. They made their way to Atlanta and melted into the city.

As Mattie was told years later, Cece wrote a letter to her father George from Chattanooga and told of the birth of her first daughter, which was Mattie's grandmother. She never heard back but learned from relatives that Mr. Buckhead had died and left the plantation to his three sons and George. That was the last they heard for years, and Cece and Boomer were afraid that it was a trick to get them back to the Buckhead Plantation.

Mattie was born in Chattanooga, and her mother, Wilma, could tell her little of her heritage, only that people said her family had money at one time.

Mattie married Rupert Brown, and they moved to Slabtown, which was a collection of renter houses thrown together for the laborers building Watts Bar Dam, near Springo. Rupert was killed in a construction accident, and Mattie bought the rundown house in Sandtown on the banks of Piney River from the settlement money she collected from the accident.

Lloyd went to the storage room at the rear of the grease rack and pulled out his chair. The special chair was kept out of sight so Moon could select his visitors, and if you were offered a chair, you felt special.

"Where's your truck?" Moon asked before his friend could settle into his seat.

"Around back at Bear's garage," replied Lloyd.

Bear Harrison was the best mechanic between Knoxville and Chattanooga. Maybe that's why his son, Jimmy, had the fastest Ford in town.

"What's wrong with it?" Moon asked.

"Well… it's missin.' Probably needs plug wires. Its got new plugs, and I'd already put wires on it, but I'm a missin' the cash to put new ones on it." Lloyd laughed. "Bear'll fix her. He always does. He's a gooden," he added with a positive nod of his head.

"Lloyd, we need to figure out a way to make us some

money. We're always a little short," Moon replied as he grinned.

"Well, you could sell your bottle collection," answered Lloyd.

"Bring a couple hundred at best. I'm talkin' about real money, where I could set back and not have to be in this hot box on ninety-five-degree days," the big man complained.

"Go play for the governor again, or at least call in some of the favors you've done for these politicians, playing at all their affairs," Lloyd offered.

"Well, the sheriff offered me a deputy job. I'm doing better than that here. And the governor said he'd help me get a foreman's job with the highway department. Done been there, done that, standing on hot asphalt instead of setting here on my butt. No, I mean big money," Moon sighed as the sweat continued down his forehead and off the tip of his nose.

"Rob a bank."

"Now you're talkin,' I think we could pull that off," Moon grinned from ear to ear.

"Yea, you just do that, lone ranger. I'm not Tonto, but I'll visit you if you go to the big house—play cards, eat, sleep, play cards; sounds like the best way for you." Lloyd laughed, flipped open the blade on his case, and began cleaning his fingernails.

Bear walked around the corner with two inches of cigar showing out of the corner of his mouth, about the same length it was at nine that morning. Pushing the door back, he delivered the news, "Lloyd, you got a burnt valve or two big bucks!"

As Lloyd looked at the ceiling, Bear looked at Moon

with a quick wink from the eye that wasn't squeezed almost shut with the cigar.

"How much?" Lloyd asked.

"Pack of Tampa Nuggets! I fixed the plug wire, now get that piece of junk out of my way," Bear growled.

"Thanks, Bear, I'm going home to Mama! You'll get them cigars first thing in the morning," a grinning gravedigger said as he walked out into a slight evening breeze.

As Bear followed Lloyd out the door, Moon said, "Let's rob a bank, Bear."

"Grow up, Moon!" Bear replied, switching the sides of his mouth where the cigar resided.

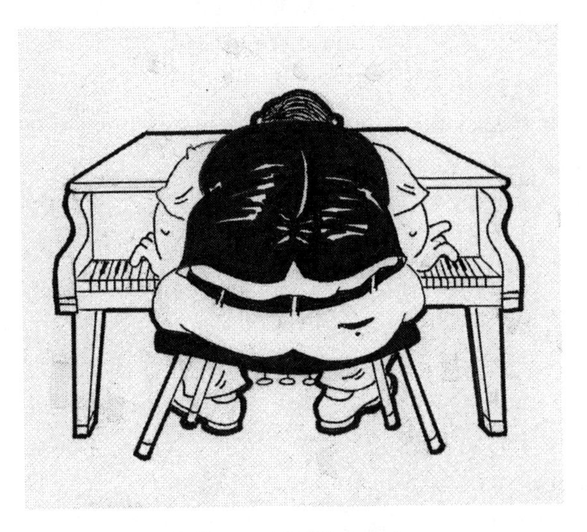

New Wheels

As summer slowly slid into fall, Hubert and Lesiel started straying from home more frequently. Granny was upset by the gradual change in their habits, but after fussing about it for a spell, she gave up.

She told Moon that the boys were growing up. Well, the big guy felt it was long overdue. The pair had saved their money and purchased a real sharp '55 Chevy with a bad motor.

That was the start of an ordeal that drove Moon, and everyone that ever knew the boys, crazy. They decided they would rebuild it themselves. They had no idea. Moon worried every time the boys checked someone's oil or added air to their tires... rebuilding an engine? Oh boy!

They got permission to use the parking area of the vacant building next to the station, that way they could continue to help Moon and work on the Chevy too. With the help of local dead beats (as Moon called them), they started taking the Chevy engine apart. This drew the hot rod crowd like spilled milk at a house fly convention. This had to stop. Cars pulled in at every angle, glass bottles and cans to clean up in the mornings. Moon was not a happy camper.

As he pulled into his station on a Monday morning, he observed a puddle of a black substance next to his pumps with a narrow stream coming from the boys' '55 Hell car. Their timing couldn't have been worse, as Hubert and Lesiel arrived at the station.

A Gomer Pyle. "Goll-ly," came from Lesiel, "that pan must have a hole in it."

"That's it. That's it... enough. Enough is enough," Moon squalled. Red faced and ready to explode, Moon turned and nearly ran head-on into Bear.

"Calm down, Moon, calm down, big guy. Those boys don't have anybody to help them out. I got two boys, and I'd hate for them to grow up without a mama and daddy. Hubert, get your truck, and you boys pull it round back. I'll be back there in a minute, and we'll put it in the garage," Bear ordered.

"Okay, Bear. Okay, Bear," the pair answered.

As the pair hooked up their car, Bear followed Moon into the office.

"I'm going to build that engine when they get the parts. Well, I'll have to order them. All you need to do is to tell them you need them over here... all the time," Bear growled.

"Why, Bear? It would be a good time for you to help them learn a trade," Moon needled.

"You want the car back here, Moon?" Bear snapped as he walked out the door. "Just keep running your mouth," he didn't have to wait for an answer. Bear was one of the very few that could talk tough to Moon and get away with it.

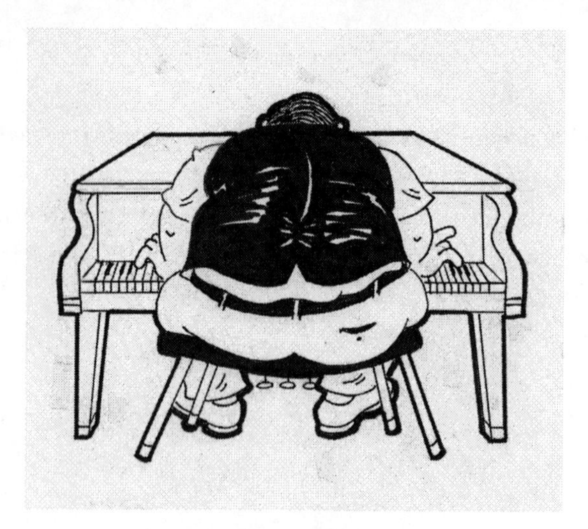

Home to Betty Jo

As Moon prepared to close the station for the day, he pulled out a small flip-top cooler and placed inside it a half bag of ice from the icebox in front of the store. Noticing it was getting low; he made a mental note to call Howard Pitman to bring enough ice to fill the box in the morning. He plopped the cooler beside him in the front seat and drove half block north to the Double-Q Drive-in. Now every Springo native knew how to defend the jokes about their drive-in. The Double-Q referred to quality, a trademark at the establishment.

As Joie, the curb hop neared Moon's Lincoln, she asked, "The usual, Moon?"

"No, it's hot. Make that two cherry shakes and one chocolate nut sundae with extra nuts . . . Betty Jo likes lots of nuts on her sundaes; three large hamburgers, two all the way and one no onions. Now, if ol' H.B. is not looking, throw an extra slab of meat on two of the burgers and hurry, the air on this thing hasn't gotten cold yet," Moon concluded.

seventy years old and had retired as president of Pioneer Bank in Chattanooga but continued as chairman of the board even after moving to Rhea County. He had bought several acres of land on the Tennessee River and built a six-bedroom mansion for himself and Tammy.

Tammy, in her late twenties to early thirties, had been married to R.M. for five years. Moon had labeled her as a looker, and rightfully so. As the couple attended their first event at the Milligan residence, Tammy made quite an impression. Mrs. Milligan and her husband, Moon, had conflicting opinions. Betty Jo was not alone; she had the support of every wife or girlfriend that ever showed at a Moon event. Let's just say the men kept an eye on Tammy.

As the evening moved on, the pattern became obvious. Tammy would put a hand on Moon's shoulder and lean forward until they were cheek to cheek. Bob and R.M. would laugh. Betty Jo had seen enough. She moved in behind Moon and, with a sharp elbow, sharp fingernails, and probing grip into the big man's neck muscles, let him know that she was in control. The smiles were gone, and Moon shifted to a slow number, and Tammy and R.M. took the dance floor.

Susanne danced only once with her husband and seemed uncomfortable with the party. Bob continued to spend a lot of time real close to Tammy.

Moon always was observant as he played. He enjoyed watching his audience, probably more than they him. He had noticed Bob's attention to Tammy but felt the banker was just a little tipsy.

Down to Georgia

Bright and early, real bright, real early (it was before nine), Moon was having a hard time. Well, let's call it adjusting this particular Sunday morning after the late night party.

The ringer on his phone was having diarrhea. Finally, "What?" he growled.

"Moon, Bill. Wanted to get a hold of you before leaving for church. Been trying since Friday evening!" the old friend reported.

It was a quick flashback for Moon. Sunday morning, Springo Methodist Church, Bill and his mother, bad headache.

"No … no … no … call me after noon," *clunk* … Moon ended.

Bill knew Moon's moods and got in touch later. He had told friends that he worked with in the research department at Lockheed about the big guy. They had listened to the tales of Moon and his musical accomplishments. The department manager, Mr. Sewart, was a retired air force man that had joined the army before the air force had completely became a separate entity.

Mr. Sewart had been around for quite a while but no one knew his age, and no one would dare ask. To his face, he was known as Mr. Sewart, but in his absence, he was R.C.

R.C.'s wife was quite a social player in the North Atlanta circles. It had Bill checking out the Atlanta Sunday Journal to see if Sibyl was hosting or attending a charity or social event. She was the first person any of the Lockheed guys knew that traveled in those circles. Sibyl decided that she wanted to throw a party for all of those working for R.C., all forty some odd and their spouses. We found out later that R.C. fought the idea with all his worth, but as usual, Sibyl won out. She immediately started talking about entertainment—formal dancing, classical music, and possibly a violinist. It was her chance to take the working class people and expose them to new and exciting experiences.

The former pilot had enough. He shot her down, and there wasn't any doubt that Sibyl realized that it was time to negotiate.

"Okay, R.C. What do you suggest?" she inquired.

"Let the fellows at the lab come up with something," he firmly answered.

A shiver ran up her spine. Oh, this could be terrible, as visions of the Beverly Hillbillies flooded her mind. Why, she remembered R.C. telling of one of his men from Dahlonega, Georgia, up in the mountains, being a state trooper but getting fired for hauling moonshine. This could be a disaster. What if Mrs. Pinksly or Mrs. Atkins got wind of this, they would never attend one of her gala events again. The time and details of remodeling their southern mansion ... oh my! Oh my!

Well now, R.C.'s foot was down, and it stayed down. The next morning, he called in his lab supervisor and told him to get with his people and decide on the entertainment.

"Well, Mr. Sewart, we may already have that decided. Bill, you know the young technician from Tennessee?" the supervisor asked.

R.C. nodded yes.

"He's been talking about this young man he grew up with. He sounds like a real piano player, been on the Opry in Nashville, plays for all the politicians, even the governor, I think," he reported.

"Ha! Ha! The governor. Hmmm ... wonder what Sibyl will think now!" R.C. said to himself.

All the details were worked out, and Moon was happy with the money the group had offered. He and Betty Jo would drive down to Kennesaw on Friday evening and stay with Bill and his family.

The big bash was set for Saturday night, but on Saturday at noon, it was time for Moon's visit to the Rio-Vista Restaurant on US-41, just south of Marietta. It would be the big man's third visit, and the manager probably came down with a migraine at the sight of Moon. All you can eat! Fried catfish and frog legs! Bill had concerns of the big man's ability to perform after his devastating afternoon food intake at the restaurant. No problem, Moon was a pro, he could survive the onslaught of a food bar anytime, anywhere, any amount, and perform as expected. He was a pro.

As they drove up the winding, dogwood-lined

driveway to the gleaming white, two-story mansion, with it's six white columns, Moon smiled.

"Well, Willie, you've done it this time. Bigger than the governor's," he admired. As Moon exited the automobile, he tried to get one, just one, button on his favorite baby blue and gold sequined coat to button. It wasn't even close. He grinned as he asked Betty Jo, "Honey, did you take my coat up since last weekend?"

"Right, Moon. Try the folks down at the catfish place, I think they had something to do with it," Betty Jo deadpanned.

As they were greeted by their hosts, there was an obvious difference in their demeanor. R.C. with a big handshake, pat on the back, and a smile; and Sibyl with her face screwed to one side as if the prunes she had obviously consumed were tainted, as Moon would later whisper. She suddenly stepped to one side and dropped her hand slightly short of Moon's outstretched hand. In her defense, she was possibly preparing to defend herself in case there was an attack! You see, the bottom three buttons on Moon's powder blue silk shirt were under extreme duress, and maybe she realized the big man had not exhaled since he entered the door.

Unaffected, Moon took another step toward the hostess, "You ready to rock and roll, mama?" Moon asked.

The group standing around the formal entranceway dropped their jaws in silence, even ol' war tested R.C. was ready for a full retreat. As Sibyl turned abruptly and quickly began her escape, she snapped, "R.C., show them in."

As Moon was shown to the piano and softly started to play, he whispered to Betty Jo, "Hun, get me a Coke."

This was code for alcohol, normally reserved for late

in his gig or if he wasn't really feeling comfortable with his audience.

He opened with a couple of old reliables, slow and easy. Sibyl, from a distance, seemed to smile and sway slightly. Then Moon suddenly came down full tilt with both hands on the keys with "Shake, Rattle, and Roll." Straight to the bar went Miss Sibyl. She quickly had a view of the bottom of her glass. The hostess remained at her post for the next hour and a half.

"Hey, Moon, do you know 'Whole Lotta Lovin'"?" a voice inquired.

Moon felt a hand on his shoulder and glanced up to see the hostess with a silly grin on her face. He immediately moved into "Whole Lotta Lovin'" without missing a key.

"Hey, hostess with the mostess, why don't you go around there and hop up on the piano so we can make eyes, putty cat?" he said as he slid into "Ain't that a Shame."

With a giggle that had been dormant for thirty years, she complied. Two hours later, she was singing off key, loudly, and several bars behind. When she tried to stand and dance on the piano, R.C. decided she had gone too far and was quickly becoming an embarrassment; it was time to take her upstairs. As R.C. started toward her, she ordered him to get back and leave her alone, the piano man played on. R.C. continued to approach, and she took off her left high heel and reared back like a mighty warrior. As the shoe tumbled through the air, it curved high and outside. *Smash* ... into the large plate glass window, little spider-like lines began at the epicenter of the contact point and spread through its entirety ... the piano man played on!

Boys and Toys

On Monday morning, Moon slid out of the seat of his old Jeep and ambled around the side of the station and came face to face with Lloyd, his latest trade in hand. He handed a shiny pocket watch with matching gold chain to Moon.

"Got it, Moon, been trying to trade ol' Sam out of it for a year," Lloyd said, glowing with pride.

"Keep good time?" Moon growled.

"Yep. Says here you're thirty minutes late."

"Awe, been down to Georgia," Moon grumbled inaudibly as he fumbled for the key to the front door.

"Did you hear any dueling banjoes?" the gravedigger asked laughing.

"Hubert and Lesiel already been by this morning," Lloyd continued, still amused at his own humor.

"What did they want?" Moon asked grumpily.

"They wanted to see how your trip went and to show you their new paint job on the '55, you ol' grump. Those boys are the best friends you got, give them a break," Lloyd scolded.

As Moon deposited start up money in the cash register, Hubert and Lesiel pulled up and stopped right in front of the door.

"Hey, Moon, how'd your trip go? Have a bunch of people hear you? Make a lot of money? What did you sing? Did you sing any Elvis songs?" the boys fired.

"Wow! Whose '55 Chevy is that?" Moon asked, ignoring their questions.

"It's ours. Mr. Ellis painted it for us. Bear said he traded work, and all it cost us was for the paint, pretty ain't it?" Hubert answered.

"Sure is, boys," Moon replied.

"If you don't need us today, Mrs. Johns wants us to come down and work for her the next couple of days, but if you need us, we'll call and tell her we can't make it," Lesiel explained.

"Lloyd, can you get hold of Carl?" Moon asked.

"Yea, he'll work. Talked to him last night, was going to work around the house today."

Moon's attention shifted to the pumps as his banker friend pulled up. The big guy turned and walked between Hubert and Lesiel.

"Boys, I'll talk to you in a minute, don't run off. Oh, Bob, what are you doing here on a Monday morning?" the big guy curiously inquired.

"Oh, I've got to go to Chattanooga for a meeting. Be gone all morning. Need anything?" he thoughtfully asked.

Moon responded with, "No, nothing that can't wait.

Thinking about adding a room at the house, restructuring my loan, you know."

"I will get with you first thing tomorrow, Buddy," Bob answered.

"Good enough. Have a good day!" Moon replied.

Moon stopped and leaned into Lesiel's side of the Chevy as the boys were ready to go.

"I need you boys back here by four. Jerry Henderson needs a set of tires on his car... okay?" Moon stated.

"Shur, Moon. We'll be back by then, if not before," Hubert stated as he revved his engine.

Lloyd was gone for most of the morning but stopped by about lunchtime with bologna, cheese, bread, and all the fixings. Carl was real good help, so Moon was in for an easy day. Every time Carl was out of the office, Moon would bring up his plans to hit the bank.

"Moon, if you keep on talking about robbing the bank, people will start believing you might actually rob it," Lloyd informed.

"I've not talked about it to anyone except you, Lloyd. I think we can pull it off! We can do it without setting foot inside the door," Moon explained.

"You're crazy. What are you going to do, get Hubert and Lesiel to do it for you?"

"Well, they will be used but won't know anything about it," Moon replied.

Lloyd grinned as he said, "You really been thinking

about this? Think you got it all figured out? How much you think you'd get?"

"We'd get, Lloyd! You and me, fifty-fifty," the big man said as he leaned forward and looked Lloyd straight in the eyes.

Ding, Ding—the silence was broken.

"Better hustle out there, Moon, Mrs. Hawthorn will want you to pump her gas."

"She's a nice lady, Betty Jo and I think the world of Susanne. She's a good friend," Moon said.

"Hey, Sue, what's a nice lady like you doing in a place like this?" Moon kidded.

"Well, I've got to pay some bills and get some groceries. Just thought I'd get some gas before I go home," the lady said in a somber tone.

"Jo and I missed you at our last get together. Bob said you were sick. Jo hasn't been able to get you on the phone. What's going on? Have you been sick, Sue?"

Before Sue could speak, Betty Jo pulled up by the station, parked, and got out of her car.

"I've paid the bills, Moon. Now make some more money and I'll buy some groceries," she kidded. "Hi, Sue, been trying to reach you on the phone, been out of town?"

Susanne began to tear up and put her hands over her face.

As Betty Jo stepped forward, Moon took his cue to head to the station.

"What's going on, Moon, Betty Jo catch you flirting with the banker's wife?" Lloyd playfully asked.

"No! I wish that was all it was. I think her husband is mistreating her," Moon quietly stated.

"Hum, why, he don't stay around enough for that. I passed him down close to Ole Washington on Highway 302 about a week ago. He was just a flying. If you or I was running like that, we'd probably get pulled over by the law or wreck or something, anyway." The gravedigger suddenly became talkative. "I've got to go see Hawthorn in a little bit to get a loan to put a new roof on the house."

"No use, he's not at the bank, he went south about an hour ago," Moon informed.

"Moon, Sue, and I are going to Crossville. She needs to get out. See you later, honey," Betty Jo said as she popped her head into the office.

"Okay, be careful on those curvy roads," Moon stated.

It was quiet as both men stood looking out as, slowly, the morning moved into the past.

"I gotta go wash the hearse," Lloyd said, breaking the silence.

"Lloyd, come by at closing time and we'll go for a ride and talk about the bank job."

"You're crazy, Moon! I got work to do!" Lloyd said as he slammed the door.

The day was busy for Moon and Carl at the station as they stayed on the front. Moon didn't do lube jobs or tires when he didn't have three working. Most of the regular customers didn't seem to care though. If a tire repair was needed, they'd just take it to one of the five other full-service stations in town.

Preacher Huel Booker, from Center Baptist Church, was becoming a regular customer, and Moon was taking a cotton to him.

He told the big man, "If you're not going to the Methodist, then come on over and visit us at Center Church."

At 4:00 p.m. sharp, the Norfolk and Southern freight train rumbled through Springo, overtaking any audible sound in the city. Moon thought, *If I were to rob the bank at 4:00 p.m., all I would have to do would be to get the law's attention on this side of the tracks and put an ol' car in the underpass north of town. Now my plan's better!* Suddenly his thoughts were interrupted by Hubert and Lesiel.

Their arrival had been masked by the rumble of the southbound Southern.

"Boys, you got back right on time. S.E.'s not got here yet, but he should be over shortly," the boss informed.

"I thought you said Jerry Henderson?" Hubert questioned.

"S.E.'s just a nickname. It's Mr. Henderson, boys," Moon clarified.

"Oh, Moon! Mr. Hawthorn beat us down there this morning," Lesiel declared.

"What are you talking about?" Moon asked.

"Well, you know he was here gettin' gas this morning, and ah, and ah, when we got to Miss Tammy's, his car was there!" Lesiel excitedly reported.

"Boys, he was going to Chattanooga, told me so

this morning, must have ridden with Mr. Johns," Moon informed.

"No! No!" Hubert exclaimed. "He must've been helping Miss Tammy with her bills or something, cause we saw him in the kitchen with her. Moon, when we got ready to come home, we went to put our tools in the shed around back, his car hadn't moved all day."

"Damn!" Moon exclaimed as he hit the counter with his hand.

"Something wrong, Moon?" Hubert asked.

"Nah ah, here comes Jerry, guide him into the rack and take his tires off and break them down. I'll show you the new ones to put on!" Moon ordered.

In spite of the stress he felt from the Hawthorn situation, Moon was always ready for a laugh. Once again at the expense of Hubert and Lesiel. Moon could be cruel.

"Fellas, look right here at the top of the tire. Hubert, pay attention! You must have the top of the tire on top when you put on a set of tires, understand-o?" Moon kidded.

"Which is the top? I can't tell on a tire. Is it where they got the name ov' 'em? They're round, you know, Moon," Lesiel questioned.

"Aw, boys, I put an X on each tire with this chalk, now make sure it's on top... okay?" Moon explained, all for Jerry's enjoyment.

As the boys finished with the tires, Jerry and Moon sat to discuss the world situation all the way down to Springo and were still a long way from solving any major problems. Jerry started telling stories of duck hunting the past season. Mackie Brown, Jimmy Harrison, and Larry McCuistion were his regular hunting buddies. His favorite was Ted Thedford; as a retired navy lieutenant, he had some great war stories.

Ted hunted with all of them from time to time. His eyesight was starting to fail, so he used his navy binoculars until the fowl got close in range.

Moon didn't hunt but enjoyed hearing of their adventures with Ted.

Moon looked up and saw Susanne and Betty Jo across the street waiting for the stoplight to change. He rose and went to see what the boys were up to, as he didn't want to see Susanne. Betty Jo was standing quietly when Moon made his way back to the front of the station.

"Spend all my money?" he playfully asked.

"No, we just stopped at the Dairy Queen and then headed on back," Betty Jo dryly reported. "I think I'm going to head on home and fix some supper," she said as she walked out the door.

As Moon arrived at home, Betty Jo was sitting on the couch.

"What's up, Jo?" Moon asked as he walked in the house. "Sue told me that Bob said he didn't love her anymore. He said she never went anywhere with him and had let herself go. He told her he didn't want a divorce because it might affect his position at the bank and that would affect them both adversely. Moon, she told me she had never loved anyone but Bob, he's her whole life," Betty Jo emotionally shared. "Honey, I want you to move our home and business banking accounts to Rockwood."

"No, now's not the time, Jo. Just let me handle it."

"Don't you get in trouble, Moon. You know your temper will get you into trouble."

"What's for supper, Jo?" Moon asked, trying to change the subject.

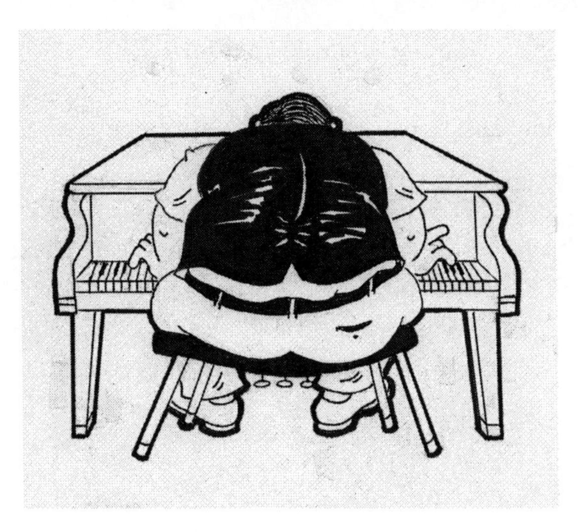

Moon to the Rescue

Moon woke earlier than normal and hadn't slept well at all. He had the Hawthorn situation on his mind. Moon was one that felt he could fix any problem, even if it wasn't his doing.

It was like the time Will Norris and his wife, Mabel, got into an argument and Will threw her car keys on top of their office building. Will had a car lot on Highway 68, north of Springo, and Mabel ran the office and kept books. Will was known to go on a bender every now and then. Well, this was then, and he was drunk as a skunk. Mabel had been to Crossville to visit a sick family friend in the hospital. She had left the lot at about six o'clock, and Will and Herb, Will's number one mechanic and a graduate of Shade-tree University, were in the shop. Seems Will had gotten a real deal on a late model Chevy down at the Dalton, Georgia, auction. He had plans for it to be a front line attraction. It had developed a knock the second time Will had taken it to the Double-Q to pick up lunch and well... show it off.

As Mabel passed the car lot, she noticed all of the lights were still on inside and out. As she turned around and headed back to the lot, she saw the shop roll-up door at the back was up and all of the shop lights were brightly shining. Mabel pulled her Mustang right up to the door and hopped out, leaving the car running. As she entered, she saw Herb with a wrench in one hand, a cigarette in the other, and five empty Budweiser cans on the fender of the car; he had the hood up on the Chevy, and he was working away.

Will was sitting on the greasy workbench in his dress pants with grease and oil all over his light blue dress shirt.

"Will! You've ruined your good clothes, and Herb, you've turned over the drain pan, oil's running everywhere!" Mabel screamed.

"Oops," Herb giggled. He didn't have to worry about the floor when he worked on cars at his house on Possum Trot Road.

"We don't have to listen to this crazy woman, Herb! Let's go get some beer," Will loudly ordered.

"I'm going home, Will. You had better lock this place up. I'll get the lights," Mabel ordered.

As they completed their tasks and ended up outside the shop, Will realized he didn't have a vehicle to drive.

"I'm going to take the Mustang. I can't drive that damn Chevy," Will announced.

Will battled with Mabel for the keys as they were pulled from the ignition and dropped in the floor. Will grabbed them, scrambled out of the car, and heaved them onto the roof of the shop.

"You fool. Now neither of us have a car! Give me the

keys to the building, and I'll get a car off the lot," she ordered.

"No, no, no," Will teased. "I've got a ride. Come on, Herb, we'll go in your pickup." As they spun out of the lot, the truck threw gravel on the cars.

Mabel surveyed her situation. She had left her business key ring on her desk before she went to Crossville. It had so many keys on it that she didn't want to lug it around inside the hospital. Big mistake! Now what?

She'd walk down to Dodson's Grocery Store; it wasn't that far. She could find someone to take her home.

"No, might run past Will on the way, and he would go crazy, drunk and all," she thought. "Oh, I've got it. I can call Moon or Betty Jo, they know how to handle Will when he's been drinking." Mabel remembered the time Will showed himself at one of Moon's parties. Moon took Will's gun after Will threatened to pull it out of his waistband; Moon slapped him across the face with it and then emptied the bullets into the trashcan. Moon took Will home, came back to the party, and played like nothing had ever happened. Moon told Mabel to tell Will to come see him when he sobered up and he'd give him his gun back. Later, he told Will that if he ever found out that he'd hit Mabel, he'd come stomp a mud hole in his butt. Moon had a way with words.

I'll call Moon, Mabel decided.

"Betty Jo, this is Mabel. Will's drunk again. He threw the keys to my Mustang on top of the office. Can Moon come get me and take me home?" she asked.

"Does he have his gun, Mabel?" Betty Jo questioned. "No, it's probably in that Chevy he's been driving. It's got a bad motor. He just bought it. That's what this is all about. He's with Herb. He's always drinking. We need to fire him!" Mabel replied.

"Mabel! You need to just get on home; Herb's not your problem! I'll send Moon up to the lot," Betty Jo stated.

"No, I'm up at Dodson's Grocery Store, and thanks, Jo," Mabel said as she calmed.

It was nearing 10:00 p.m., and Dodson's was closing for the night. Mabel stepped out front when Dan Sharp, a neighbor that lived on the same street as the Milligans and she and Will, walked out.

"Got trouble, Mabel? Need a ride?" Dan asked.

"No. I'm waiting on someone, thanks," Mabel replied.

As Dan hurriedly drove off in his new black Buick, Moon arrived to pick up Mabel. He started to lecture her about Will.

"Moon, I'm tired. I don't want to get into that now," Mabel ended.

As they got to the Norris home, Moon waited as Mabel retrieved her house key from her super secret hiding place—under the mat.

When Moon got home, he plopped down into his chair. Jo asked if he was going to watch the TV or go to bed, but before Moon could answer, the phone rang.

"I know you're having an affair with Will Norris's wife, and he'll shoot you if he gets a call to tell him you were with her tonight. He's riding with Herb looking for her. I've got people watching you. You just took her home," the mysterious, barley audible, mumbling voice said. "Now, listen carefully. Take five hundred dollars and put it in a shoebox, tie a string around it, take it to the Southern Style Motel, and place it in the phone booth next to the road by the pool," the voice ordered.

"I don't have five hundred dollars, you idiot, and I don't know if I have a shoe box either ... wait. Honey, do we have an empty shoe box?" Moon asked as he toyed with the caller.

"You got two hundred and fifty?" the bad guy asked.

"Wait, let me see," Moon said as he messed with the really dumb, really bad guy.

Moon looked at a puzzled Betty Jo, and with a really big grin on his face, he started counting; "Twenty, forty, sixty, eighty, one hundred, a hundred and twenty ... oh, here's a fifty. Let's see ... one seventy, one eighty, one ninety, two hundred ... let's see, what's Betty got in her purse ... wow! Now, two twenty, two forty, two sixty ... oh, you only wanted $250.00, right?" Moon snickered.

"Don't get smart with me. You just put it in a shoebox and deliver it to the phone booth at eleven sharp, then get back into your car and drive south to the junction. Pull off the highway and wait fifteen minutes. No tricks! You got it?" the man with the plan asked.

"Yea, does it matter if it's a men or women's shoebox?" Moon inquired.

"Don't get smart with me, or I'll call Will now! I got people watching," he nervously answered.

"Okay, okay, sorry. I'll be there. Please don't tell Will."

Moon turned to Betty Jo. "Get me a shoebox and some of that nylon string from the pantry. Honey, oh yea, I need a clothes hanger too!"

"What's going on?"

"Some nut's playing games with me," Moon answered as he walked over to his desk to retrieve his thirty eight special and slipped it into his jacket pocket.

As he prepared the box for the drop, he explained the phone call to Jo.

"Moon, I don't think this is a prank! Don't go," she pleaded.

"Well, it's a nut, and I can take care of it. Call Mabel and tell her I'll pick her up in a minute," he ordered.

As she reached for the phone, she said, "Please don't go! Why get

Mabel involved—" Slam*!* Moon was on his way, stopping only at the Norris's to pick up Mabel, and they sped toward town.

Mabel responded differently than Betty Jo.

"Let's go get Will and let him take care of it. His gun is at the shop," she told Moon as they drove toward town.

"He's drunk, and I sure don't need him," Moon snapped. Moon cruised by the motel and on up to his station, made a U-turn, and eased back down to the phone booth. He attached the clothes hanger to the shoebox and secured the box to the phone and cord. He then slowly pulled his Lincoln onto Highway 27 and headed south, his eyes affixed to the rearview mirror. He saw no sign of headlights at the motel. As he approached the last station leaving town, he cut his lights off, made a U-turn, and coasted in behind the Texaco station's pumps. Moon tried to stay off his brakes to avoid the illumination of his taillights. Slowly, he applied his emergency brake, as if this was a daily practice. He and Mabel sat silently, watching the phone booth about one hundred yards away. Finally, a pair of headlights came down the highway and passed right by the drop sight. It proceeded south and passed the Texaco and then disappeared into the night. As they looked back toward the motel, headlights were turning in and slowly pulled to the side of the phone booth.

"It looks like a dark car... maybe a Cadillac or Pontiac," Moon whispered as if his voice could be heard at the booth. After several nervous moments, the door opened. Moon immediately started the Lincoln and slipped into gear. He was in luck. There was not a car to be seen in either direction. He quickly sped toward the motel.

"It's a black Buick," Moon exclaimed as he drew closer.

"It's Dan Sharp! It's Dan Sharp!" Mabel screamed.

Moon would recall later, as he told Betty Jo of the escapade, that it was like everything was in slow motion. Sharp was wildly jerking at the box, trying to free it from the clutches of the clothes hanger and nylon cords. As the Lincoln drew closer to the booth's door, Moon slammed on the brakes. As the big, really big, man in the really big car slid closer, the extortionist turned to look over his shoulder, refusing to let go of the treasure box full of newspaper. His eyes were bulging, his veins were about to pop, and his mouth looked as if it could swallow a football. *Bam!* The Lincoln slammed into the phone booth, breaking it loose from its anchor bolts and tilting it to the rear.

Ol' Dan was hanging on for dear life. Moon slowly lifted his foot from the brake and slowly moved his foot to the gas pedal and even more slowly, *oh* so slowly, applied pressure. The booth squeaked and cracked as the pieces of glass fell to the ground.

"Stop, Moon! Stop! Please stop! I'm sorry!" Dan begged.

The big man reacted by giving the gas pedal one more little wiggle. *Pow!* The booth's rear bolts let go, and the telephone booth toppled to the ground on cue from the screaming man inside. Moon flipped the Lincoln-made bulldozer into reverse and then pulled away.

Moon crossed the tracks and headed up Highway 68.

"Where are you going, Moon?" Mabel asked.

"To pick up a drunk and take him home."

As they pulled to the back of the car lot, the light shone out of a half opened door. Moon told Mabel to stay in the car as he opened his door; he walked to the sliding door and peered in. He slowly turned to Mabel and motioned for her to come on. He needed her help. As she looked inside, she began to laugh. Moon didn't think it was funny; two drunks passed out on the floor.

"Well, let's open the door and I'll pull my car in. You need to get your keys out of the office and find his gun and give it to me," Moon ordered.

As Mabel went into the office, the big kid walked over to the water cooler with an empty beer can and filled it with ice water, turned, walked over to Herb, and emptied the entire can of water on his head. He thrashed his arms, spit and spewed, and looked at Moon.

"Hi, Moon, whaaat ya do... do... doin'... tehehe?" Herb asked. Moon reached around Herb's neck and grabbed his shirt just below the collar and lifted the little man halfway up and drug him out to his truck, opened the door, and stuffed the mechanic inside. Then, Moon took the keys from the ignition and placed them on top of the passenger side front tire. Turning around, he walked back into the shop and repeated the procedure with Will. As he made it to the doorway, Mabel joined the exodus.

"Moon, we'll just put him in the Mustang. I got my extra set of keys out of the office safe," she explained.

"Open the back door on the Lincoln," Moon ordered.

As they completed their cargo loading, Moon ordered, "Start your car and follow me to your house!"

As the Lincoln crossed the tracks by the Shell station, Moon could see some flashing lights down the highway.

"Must have been a wreck," Moon loudly said to his passenger. With no response, the big guy broke into a thunderous laugh.

Moon's relationship with Will still hadn't gotten back to normal. It had been a couple of years, but it wasn't anything like the current problems with the Hawthorns. Dealing with a drunk was child's play compared to the situation with Robert Hawthorn.

As he drove to work, he thought of Susanne . . . poor Sue. Moon, used to fixing other people's problems, had no plan. He was in misery. Little did he know that this day would mark the beginning of the end of the current situation.

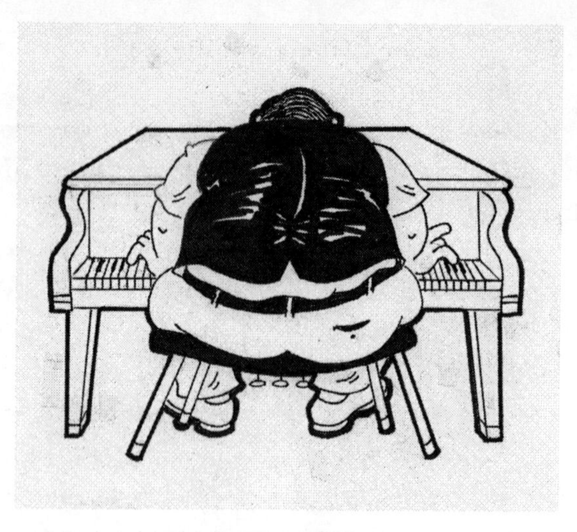

You're Fired

As he neared town, he enjoyed the first chill of the season in his Jeep. He thought that it wouldn't be long until he would put the side doors back on his ride. His thoughts of season change cleared his mind, and as he unlocked his front door, he was humming a tune. It had been a while.

He would be playing the next three weekends at political events, all for incumbents. They were the best, as far as Moon was concerned; they had deep pockets.

Moon closed the cash register after he finished putting in the seed money for the day. A vibrating noise was audible before its cause became visible. Someone had a problem. Well, it was a '55 Chevy... Hubert and Lesiel's '55 Chevy. The tail pipe was dragging, and the muffler was dangling. It looked like it had come in last at a mud bogging race. As Hubert shut it off with a grin on his face, he asked, "Hey, Moon, can we put her in the bay and clean her up?"

Before the big man could get his question out, he got the answer.

"We took her huntin' last night out on the mountain, got stuck on a loggin' road way back in 'ere," Hubert explained.

"Why in the world would you take your Chevy hunting? You've got a truck, you idiots!" Moon screamed.

Hubert threw his head back, proud as could be, as he smartly answered, "We were spotting deer, and if you get one, you don't carry it around in the back of your truck or the game warden will see it... so there!"

"There... there's the highway! Get your butts back into your junker and don't come back! So there!" a red faced Moon ordered, as he angrily turned and walked back into the station.

Lloyd had been watching the goings on from the station corner. As the deer hunters sped off, Lloyd started to enter the station and was nearly bowled over. Moon brushed by to wait on a customer that had driven up. It was Springo's only dentist, Dr. Leonard. He and Moon had quickly become friends after the tooth man's arrival the previous year. Lloyd nervously fiddled with his latest trade, a 1903 railroad watch. Soon, Moon entered the station and was startled to see his friend.

"Where did you come from?" Moon asked.

"I was two feet from you when you ran off the best friends you've ever had," Lloyd answered.

"I've had it with those two. Everybody tries to help 'em. Mr. Ellis painted their car, Bear rebuilt the motor, I put tires on it, and they don't appreciate anything!" the big guy complained as his slumped into his chair.

The happy tune, ambushed by real life, and he sat motionless. The gravedigger stood uncomfortably, looking out at the little town, and yawned. The start of another day.

Sometimes looking down isn't all that bad. Now, we're not just talking about finding loose change. As Moon examined the hairline cracks in the worn cement floor of the station, his eyes wandered to the gravedigger's shoes. Wingtip! New, dress wingtips! As his view slowly moved up, he saw stiffly starched, church-going overalls leading to a blue dress shirt.

"Lloyd! Are you digging a grave or preaching at a funeral today?' Moon inquired.

"No, I told you I was going to see Hawthorn today and get some money to do work on the house," he calmly replied.

"Oh, well, you look real nice," Moon answered. "By the way, I'll need Carl for a couple of days till I figure out what to do about some help here at the station," Moon continued.

"His car is down. I've got time to run out to his house and pick him up. I'll drop him off on my way to the bank," Lloyd stated.

As Carl changed oil and lubed a couple of cars, Moon waited on the customers at the front. Ray Keylon, Moon's favorite teacher and coach from Springo High, drove through and asked if Lloyd was around.

"He should be back soon. He had some business to take care of," Moon informed Ray as he leaned against his high-test pump.

"You tell that gravedigger that I traded for an ol' Winchester riffle he would really like. I've got to get back to school, but I will see him this weekend," the coach relayed.

As the coach drove off, Moon shifted his weight and looked into the sky. It had been a troubling time for him. Moon was oblivious to the passing traffic on Highway 27, a few feet from his pumps. He whispered an inaudible prayer and slowly began to hum. Soon, his hum turned into "Have Thine Own Way, Lord." Quietly at first, almost a whisper, then audibly, as he quietly sang, "Thou Art the Potter, I Am the Clay." As the automobiles traveled by, Moon progressed into the third verse, "wounded and weary, help me I pray."

Suddenly, his attention shifted to the railroad tracks and the sound of banging shovels and rakes, as Lloyd's ol' truck sped across the train tracks. Never had Moon witnessed his friend driving in such a manner. The seriousness of the situation became more evident as the gravedigger pulled between the gas pumps and the station door. Lloyd's truck screeched to a halt. He slammed his door and marched into the station office.

He hadn't seen Moon standing at the gas pumps, just a few feet from his truck. Lloyd never pulled in front of the station except to get gas, and he wasn't known for his rapid starts or stops. Truth is, ol' Lloyd wasn't known for rapid movement in any form. He was, in fact, a gentle person, kind of non-excitable.

"Do you know what Hawthorn did to me? He turned me down! Do you know why? Said I didn't have a credit record! Well, I've always paid my bills on time and paid cash for everything I need," Lloyd said.

"Just calm down, bankers have certain—"

"Don't tell me to calm down, Moon! Tell me how we're going to rob that bank?" Lloyd demanded with both hands on his hips.

The phone rang. Again, Moon was saved by the bell. *This should give Lloyd time to cool down a bit,* Moon thought as he placed the phone to his ear.

"Springo Shell," Moon answered.

"Hey, buddy, now would be a good time to come over and talk about what you need. Might be easier to just add it to your station loan. Save you some money up front and a little on interest. Your payment would only increase slightly," Bob rambled.

"I tried to call you yesterday. Didn't know your business was going to take you all day. I called Susanne to see if you might be home with the little woman, but she didn't have any idea where you were. I was going to tell you I had decided to wait until next spring to work on the house," the smiling big man concluded.

As the conversation ended, the dial tone softly played its musical tone into the big man's ear.

He whispered, "Gotcha!"

"What are you doing sucking up to him? You don't have to drop your loan because he turned me down. I don't need his money. I'll pay as I go and fix up my house the way that woman wants it," Lloyd said in a much quieter voice than before.

"Lloyd, listen to me! This is not about a loan. We both can wait. We've always played by the rules. We're not looking for a loan, we're going to take the money and get Hawthorn fired. Get enough on him made public. Susanne can sue for divorce and take everything he has," Moon concluded.

"What are you talking about? What could we ever get on him?"

Over the next couple of hours, between customers, Moon updated Lloyd on the evidence and his theory on Hawthorn's involvement with Tammy Johns. It appeared that Hawthorn's relationship with Tammy had heated up in the last couple of months.

At the end of Moon's talk, Lloyd simply said, "I'm not going to use a gun."

"There will be no guns. You and I will never set foot in the bank! I will promise you that," Moon explained.

"Let's do it tomorrow!" Lloyd insisted.

"No! This has to be planned one step at a time. Timing is the key. Be patient. I'll take care of you. I have to get every detail checked out. I need to know every time ol' Bob leaves Springo and when he gets back," Moon concluded.

Just when he thinks he's explained enough for the time being, a thought tumbles from the big man's brain.

"Lloyd, we can start getting ready tomorrow. I need you to do some detective work. Find out where R.M. and Tammy Johns live. You know, get a lay of the land," Moon related.

"I already know where they live, Moon. You know ol' Seth Johnson?" Lloyd asked.

"No."

"Well, now, the Johns bought the ol' Johnson home place. Seth, golly, he must be eighty! He lives on about twenty acres before you get to Miss Tammy's new house. His house has a fine ... I mean fine ... view of the little tramp's house and grounds." Excitedly, quicker than a gravedigger can dig a hole, Lloyd's personality changed to smiling, ready-to-roll inspector.

Moon tried to pull him back to earth.

"Lloyd, do you think we can trust him not to say a word. Is his eyesight and memory good enough to help us out?"

"Sharp as a tack. A little bit nosy, I think it might cost us!"

"How much?"

"Oh, some Brown Mule Twist," Lloyd answered with a smile.

Moon walked over and opened a cabinet.

"Got just a couple of Twists left. I'll order an extra box. That's the cost of doing business, I guess," he mumbled.

"Takes money to rob money," the suddenly lighthearted digger said. "When are you going to tell me how we are going to rob ol' Hawthorn's Bank?"

"Don't say the words rob and bank again ... not a word!" Moon snapped back.

"Okay, okay," Lloyd stammered.

As Moon was locking the station door at the close of the day, Bear walked up.

"Why did you fire those boys? They think you hung the moon and could walk across Piney without getting wet! They're like little boys. You've given 'em advice and watched after them in a way Granny never could. You ought to be ashamed of yourself, Moon Milligan!" Bear scolded.

Moon's jaw became tight as an escaping tear ran down his face, then he just looked at the ground as Bear turned and disappeared around the corner.

The next few weeks quickly slipped by, and the pianist stayed busy. Moon hosted only one party at his home, notably absent were *friends* Bob and Susanne, probably an invitation oversight. Moon tickled the ivory in Nashville, Crossville, Dayton, and Kingston.

Lloyd had gotten with the program, busy supervising his surveillance team of one. Seth was busy lookin' and a spittin.' The old timer had surprised both Moon and Lloyd by keeping a neat, well-written log of goings and comings at the R.M. Johns III home.

Every single Thursday morning between nine thirty-five and nine forty-five, a Buick would arrive and then leave between 12:00 p.m. and 3:30 p.m. On various other occasions, and always within thirty minutes of Mr. Johns' exit, three vehicles would arrive.

The report read:

- shiny, new-looking red Ford (three visits) Sunday, Saturday, Sunday
- blue 1972 Plymouth (two visits) Tuesday and Wednesday
- Mac McCoy (four visits) all four on Mondays
- that's Sheriff McCoy in his county vehicle.

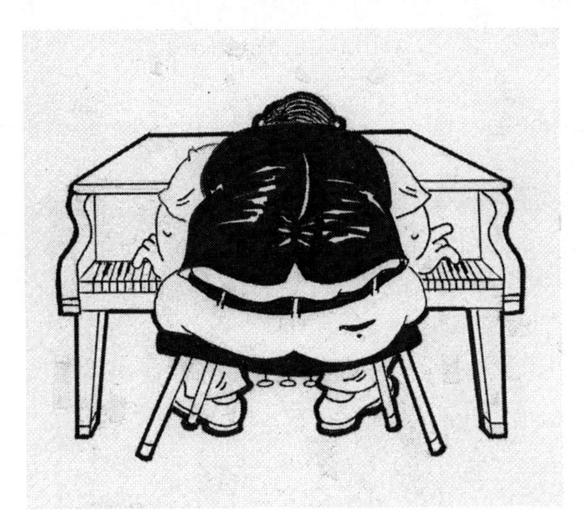

Reunion

Busy, busy Moon Milligan had a hectic couple of months. He had lost friends. Well, the banker and *friend* just didn't go together. It was Bob's doings that had caused the void. The real friends he had lost were innocent. Hubert and Lesiel had been like his children ... the ones he had not been blessed with. Even the chewing out he had gotten from Granny haunted him.

"Them boys don't have no man to show them right from wrong, and I know you have sure made a load of mistakes," Moon remembered her words. *A semi full of mistakes,* he thought as he walked to the phone and dialed the familiar numbers.

Fifteen minutes later, that ol' rattletrap truck pulled far to the side of the lot beside the station and parked. Moon had watched from the time he saw them stop at the traffic light by the post office. As they crossed the train tracks, Moon thought of the many times he had this same view. Always before it was, "Hurry up, I've got tires for you to change."

Not today. As the boys walked near the door, Moon quickly turned away and pulled out a carton of Lucky Strikes. He reached for his belt, fumbling for the key to the cigarette machine. Oh, how he wished he could see the look on their faces without turning around. If he could have his way, he would see his emotions in the mirror of their faces. Fear, sorrow, anxiety, and love... yes, a love reserved for sons returning home. Moon bit his quivering lower lip and reached for his handkerchief.

"Dern fever blister!" Moon finally broke the silence as he turned to see the boys. "How you boys been?" he said in almost a whisper.

"We've been good, Moon," Hubert declared.

"You gonna let us come back to work?" Lesiel chimed.

"You bet, fellows," Moon said as the dinger sounded from outside.

"I'll get it," Hubert declared. "It's Mr. Keylon."

"I'll wash his winders," Lesiel said with excitement in his voice. "Hi, Coach, you gonna win all the ballgames this year?"

"Oh, we'll win our share," commented Keylon as he walked into the station.

"Hi, Ray," Moon said.

"Seen Lloyd today, Moon?" questioned the coach.

"Not since about one. Guess it's about time for him to show up! Pull up a chair and wait on him."

"I'd better get home. Got to come back to town for the game tonight."

Ray Keylon had returned to Springo after completing his tour of duty with the marines. Moon had good memories of the eighth-grade teacher and coach.

On a cool, fall day, Moon was ordered to run around the block at Springo school by the young coach. Moon couldn't recall the cause for this inhuman punishment, but he was mistakenly left to circle the block at the end of the recess period. After completing a total of three trips, he stopped on the sidewalk directly in front of the coach's classroom.

The eighth grader, already a really big guy, flopped to the ground and lay on his back. Virginia Janow, a classmate, watched his play-acting with a smile, then said, "Oh! Moon's fallen down. He's passed out. Oh! He's not breathing!"

Knocking paper aside and sending his chair toppling over against the blackboard, Coach was off to save his young student.

Moon smiled as he remembered that day. The last time he was disciplined by teacher and now friend.

Before Ray was out of view, Will Norris pulled up to the gas pumps. As he strolled out to Will's car, Moon thought, *It's been over two years since the drunken incident at Will's Car Lot.*

"Good to see you, Will. Long time no see!" Moon said.

"It's all on me, Moon," he started. "I blamed you. The truth is, I've been dodging you! I'm so ashamed," Will sadly said.

"Well, Will, we all have things we would like to do over. It just shows you are man enough to come see me," Moon stated.

"No, Moon. I was not strong enough to change or come see you. I've been going to Center Baptist Church with Mabel. Preacher Booker came out to visit me three, maybe four times. Sunday I walked down the isle and accepted Jesus Christ as my Lord and Savior," Will confessed. "Moon, I know you go over to the Methodist, but are you saved, Moon?" Will asked.

"Yes, Will, just don't live like it a whole lot," Moon said.

"Moon, I'm going to be baptized Sunday out at Rhea Springs. Would you come?" Will asked.

"Will, why don't I just come to church with you Sunday? Never heard Preacher Booker," Moon answered.

"Great!"

Moon and Betty Jo arrived at Center Baptist on Sunday as the service had started. He had planned to slip in and sit on the back row. No such luck. Preacher Booker was reading the announcements as the couple moved halfway down the aisle before they found room to be seated. A low rumble emitted from the congregation as Reverend Booker looked over the top of his glasses.

"Good morning, Moon and... uh, uh... and Mrs. Moon... Betty Jo," to the snickers as he embarrassed himself.

After the preacher completed his sermon, the invitation given, Moon went down and kneeled at the altar. As the tears flowed down the big man's face, the preacher leaned over and asked, "Moon, do you know the Lord? Are you saved?" he asked.

"Yes, Preacher, I'm asking for forgiveness and guidance. I've got some decisions to make ... pray for me," Moon ended.

"I will, brother," Preacher Booker promised.

On the drive out to Rhea Springs for Will's baptism, it dawned on Moon that the fall air was already a little nippy. It was near 1:00 p.m. and still cool, awfully cool, to be going into the water.

"You know that sprinkling I got at the Methodist Church when I was saved, Betty Jo? Makes a lot of sense on a cool day, especially wading out in the lake," Moon lightheartedly said.

As Will and three others waded out into the water with Preacher Booker, the congregation standing along the bank began to clap and sing "He Leadeth Me." Moon felt tears well up in his eyes.

As Will and the others were baptized, the preacher stood and said, "There is much water." All of a sudden, Moon ran into the water like an out-of-control dump truck hitting the water. Mr. Big approached knee high, and then he lost his balance and plunged head first into the chilly water. As quick as he went under, he bobbed right back up beside the preacher.

"Ready to go under again, Moon?" the preacher asked.

"Dunk me, brother!"

On the two-mile trip back to Springo, Jo sat close to the big guy, her head resting on his shoulder. Moon was deep in thought; there was much in his life he needed to change. Surprisingly, plans for robbing a bank was not one of them.

The bank job was a mission of justice. An unfaithful, evil man must be stopped. A wonderful lady, Susanne, would be protected and freed from the banker's hold.

Thinking back to the planning of the robbery, he couldn't think of one thing he had considered seriously doing with the money. It wasn't about the money. It was evil versus good, and good would win.

Moon Milligan was on a mission.

The following Thursday, Moon took his money bag, removed the checks and large bills he had been stockpiling since Monday, and headed for Springo Bank with a purpose.

"Hi, Miss Becky," he said as he walked by Mrs. Thompson's desk outside of Mr. Hawthorn's office. "Where's the boss?"

"Oh, he had to go to his meeting in Dayton. It's every Thursday," she explained.

"Well, I hadn't seen him a lot lately," Moon replied.

"Moon, it's not personal, he said he had to spread

the bank's business around a little. He's been trading at Jerry's Esso; you know their family has been bank customers for years."

"I understand. Bob's always about the bank's business. I know all the trips to meetings in Dayton must wear him out," Moon said, struggling to hold back a snicker. "Oh! Miss Becky, what if I need to talk to him about an urgent banking problem that came up on a Thursday?" he playfully inquired.

"He doesn't want me to call. You see, we're not to talk about the meeting. They don't meet at the bank now. The meetings are somewhere else. If I called they would simply say, 'He's not here!' I know you've been told that he has a meeting every Thursday, but you've not been told what for," she concluded.

"What for, Miss Becky?" Moon played along.

Looking both directions, the loyal secretary was about to let Moon in on the *big secret.*

"Come closer," she whispered.

Moon moved closer, and Miss Becky said, "They're talking about building a branch to Springo Bank in Dayton."

"Will it be The Bank of Springo at Dayton or Dayton Bank of Springo?" Moon playfully asked.

"Well, ah ... I ... I don't know. I haven't seen anything in writing," she sputtered.

"Well, it is a secret that only Mr. Hawthorn has a feel for," Moon said.

He exchanged his checks and large bills, making a point of going to Jim Bates' window. Jim was the first male teller at Springo Bank and the youngest bank employee. Only two years out of Springo High, he was personable and always trying to please. *Little does he know, he will soon be a key in the bank heist,* Moon thought.

"Hello, Mr. Milligan! What can I do for you?" he asked.

"Give me all your cash and keep your yapper shut or I'll open up with my Tommy gun," Moon playfully said.

"Mr. Milligan, you need a half smoked cigar and one of those brimmed hats out of the thirties," he laughed.

"Jim, have a good day," Moon said as he walked out of the bank. He strolled around the sidewalk until he could see the rear of the bank and made some mental notes. Glancing at the dumpster as he turned, he viewed the roofline of Phillip's Five and Ten.

He thought, *It's time to lay out the plan with Lloyd.* As he crossed the tracks, Moon flipped his wipers on; he noticed Lloyd, Hubert, Lesiel, and Jim Riggs standing in the rain. Moon had a thought, just drive on by, just drive on by . . . but then he thought he better stop and see what was going on.

"Moon! Moon! Come here!" Lesiel called.

"I got Bristol," said Hubert as he continued holding his Coca-Cola bottle up for everyone to look at.

"But, Moon, mines farther away! I got Dalton, Georgia, and Bristol is in Tennessee . . . tell him, Moon!" Lesiel begged.

Lloyd stood to the side and grinned, as if to say, "Moon, you can't win."

"Lloyd, handle this for me," Moon said as he walked into the station to put his money in the register.

Shortly, Lloyd walked into the station. "Moon, you left me right in the middle of Springo's brain trust. I felt like the ol' wise one."

"Best I can figure, Lloyd, four idiots were standing in the rain when I drove up and it was a while before one decided to come into the dry. Ol' wise one, look forth into the siege, but for moments, you were there."

"Huh!" Lloyd says. "Oh, Moon. I meant to ask you why you wouldn't let Jim Riggs hang around here for a long time," Lloyd inquired, trying to change the subject.

"Well, you had to stay upwind from him, but he's doing better. Someone's got him bathing more often now. The biggest reason is that he bothers the customers. The final straw was when a tourist pulled up. The lady got out to go to the restroom. Jim walked around to the back of the car, looked at the tag, and asked the man, 'Where are you from?' When the fellow said 'Detroit,' Jim said to him, 'Damn liar, you're from Michigan.' When I handed him his change, his window was rolled up within an inch of the top ... *ha, ha.* Well, it's not really funny, the man was scared to death. He expected banjoes to start plunking anytime."

"Hey, Moon, Hubert said you had gone to the bank. Did you see Hawthorn?" Lloyd asked.

"It's Thursday," Moon quickly answered.

"Oh, I forgot," Lloyd said. "Well now, Mr. Johnson is right on top of everything. I talked to him yesterday and got an update," he stated.

Moon waited and waited some more. Finally, he turned and looked at Lloyd.

"Well, what's the update?"

Lloyd declared, "Hawthorn hasn't missed a Thursday since Seth started his spy assignment. However, all the others have stopped showing up, and ol' Bob has been coming down when Mr. Johns leaves every once in a while."

Moon kicked back in his cane-bottomed chair and declared, "It seems the good banker has laid down the law to his little lady. In fact, she can no longer lay down with the law! Bob-o Boy, is in total control of his assets. Let's see what we can do to upset the apple,... no, let's say the money cart," Moon and Lloyd join in a long overdue horselaugh.

"Seriously," Moon returned to the project at hand, "Lloyd, can you find a place to store one of those new trash cans I've got in the storage room at your place?"

"Sure, no problem. I'll go get one out of the storage room right now," he stated.

"No, wait until the boys go home. It's about that time now," Moon said. "Do you have an old tarp? Doesn't matter if it's got holes in it. Just got to be large enough to cover that can laid on its side in the back of a truck."

"Sure! No problem, Moon," teased the smiling gravedigger.

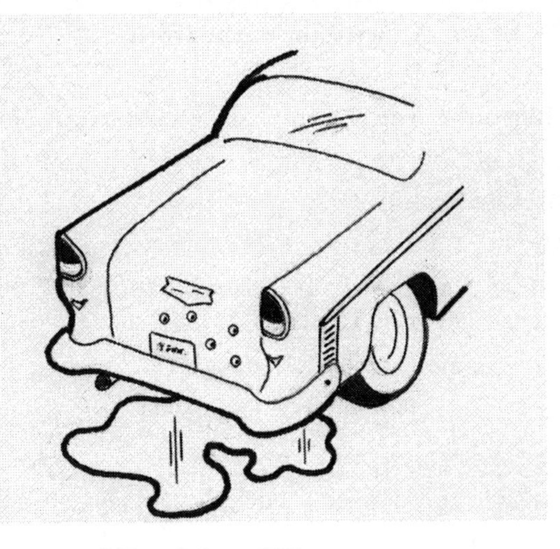

Trophy Hunters

It was mid-December. The last several weeks had been warmer than normal. The fog seldom cleared the mountain as the big guy sat next to his portable heater and peered out at the lights. Two lights on Highway 27 marched through their sequence—red, yellow, green, red, yellow, green. The stoplight by the post office was only a two-lighter—green, red, no yellow. While Moon was working for the state, he was told it was the only known light in the state that had the green light on top. Moon, one known to ponder the situation at times, figured the light did an adequate job of regulating those who wished to be regulated, and the rest . . . not.

The warm was good, but the wet that had drenched the area and bore the fog was of record-breaking amounts. Rain brought with it melancholy to Moon's spirit.

Suddenly, Hubert and Lesiel came flying into the station in their '55 Chevy and slid to a stop right in front of the door. Moon struggled to his feet, sensing this was not a normal crash landing; Hubert beat him to the door.

"Moon! We're leakin' gas! I smelt it real bad a comin' down the road. I stopped and it was a runnin' out!" Hubert stammered.

As he walked out the door, Moon could see a thin thread of liquid as it blended with the water from the morning rain. He walked around behind the Chevy and stopped cold in his tracks. Moon saw five holes in their trunk lid and said, "Boys, somebody's been shooting at you! What's going on?" The boys nervously looked at each other and started chattering at Moon simultaneously, neither even the least bit understandable.

"Hubert, drive the car around back, out in the grass beside that ol' junk tractor Bear's got back there. Lesiel, get in the station. Hubert, you stay in Bear's garage until I send Lesiel around there."

Lesiel entered the station office with Moon right on his heels.

"Lesiel, start at the beginning and tell me everything," Moon quietly spoke.

"Well, we went a huntin' last night and ah—" he started.

Moon interrupted, "You mean you were spotting deer, don't you?'

"Yea, that's right."

"I thought I told you about taking your car hunting and using your ole truck, didn't I? Say, didn't I tell you not to?" Moon lectured.

"Nope, you told us not to take the Chevy back in those loggin' roads a huntin,' and we was on Possum Trot Road up on Grandview. We went down Happy Top Road, but we didn't see none to shoot at," Lesiel explained in rapid fire.

"Lesiel, now slow down. Listen, who shot up your car, or do you even know?" Moon inquired in a quiet voice.

"Yea, I know!"

"Well, who was it?" Moon snapped as his patience was running out faster than the fuel in the gas tank.

"It was Hubert... and a... me... but... he shot it ah... three times, and I shot it just ah... two. I, ah... think."

"Why, Lesiel, why, why would you two shoot your own car?" the frustrated big man inquired.

"Well," Lesiel started slowly. "We spotted this big eight-point buck, I mean big, and Hubert, he was a drivin,' so he stopped and I slid the rifle out the winder and *bam!*"

Quicker than that deer must have fallen, Moon plopped in his chair, he had a feeling he was a ways from finding the answer to his question.

Lesiel continued, "Well, he hit the ground. I'm a tellin' you, he hit the ground deader a doorknob! So we jumped out of the car, me and Hubert, we did. Hubert was ah drivin' and ah... we grabbed him by his lags, and ah... started a draggin' him to'rd the car when we saw them lights a comin' down the road a piece. Well, Hubert said he bet it was the law and da... I'm a thinking it's the law! He's gonna get our guns and our car and a... we gonna be put rite in the middle of the jailhouse! Now Hubert, he'd been a drivin.' He goes and a gets the keys, and we stuff that thang in the trunk! Now it's heavy, and ah... ah his rack gets hung in the front of the trunk. Well now, we slam that trunk three times 'fore we get her to latch. That was a big deer. Well, we go jump in the car, and Hubert, he's ah... a drivin.' Takes off down the road lickety split without nary a light on. He was a comin' up on Tater Reed's place, and we'd been out there when we was little 'n all. Now, Hubert, he remembered down past Tater's house, there was a lane, just as you went around the curve, you could see it, it went out to the barn. Well, now we went slidin' around the curve and just barely make the turn off to the barn. Hubert, you see, he's a still a drivin.'"

Moon folded his arms and leaned back. He wasn't angry anymore. He was just trying to keep from laughing.

This guy needs to be on the Ed Sullivan Show! He's a hoot! the big guy thought. Moon was glad Hubert was still driving, because he needed Lesiel to keep on telling the story.

"Well, we pull in behind the barn, and the lights pass. We can ... ah ... see them lights in the top of the trees as it goes on down the road. Hubert, he's ah ... a drivin,' pulled out and started back up the road the way we just got dun a comin' from. Now, this was ah ... the way we wuz a comin' from before we ah ... you know, ah ... spotted the deer," Lesiel rambled on.

Now Moon, still really puzzled of how the holes got in the trunk of their car, didn't know if they were coming or going.

"All of a sudden," Lesiel exclaimed, "that deer ... it *come alive,*" he said with his eyes as big as saucers. "It was a *comin' plum* into the back seat, ah ... ah ... tryin' to get us! It was *comin' alive.* Hubert, yes, he was still driving, pulled over to the side of the road, and while he was a gettin' out, he got his gun and da ... ah ... told me to get my gun too! That thang was ah ... bangin' and a squealin' like I ain't never heard," Lesiel told with true emotions untethered even hours after the remarkable event.

"Well, now, the back of the trunk was, ah, shakin' and da bangin' and Hubert hollered, 'Shoot him, Lesiel' and I said, 'You shoot him,' and he said, 'You shoot him,' and I said—"

"Will somebody shoot the damn deer?" Moon screamed.

"He shot first, then I shot, then he shot, then I shot, and that deer was still a bangin' in the trunk, and Hubert shot again, and everything got real quiet, Moon, 'cept my ears was a ringin,'" Lesiel exhaustedly finished.

Bear walked around the corner of the station and up to the door with rain dripping off his head and mud on his knees. He was not a pretty sight.

"Bear, what have you been doing?" Moon asked.

"Oh, just checking out a gas tank. Two out of five, that's all the damage they did, but, Moon, tell me something. According to Hubert, it happened last night about eleven o'clock, and they didn't come to the station until this morning. How did it still have gas in it?" Bear asked.

"Lesiel, did you smell any gas last night?" Moon questioned.

"Yea, on the way home and when we backed up to the barn. By the time we got the deer unloaded, skinned, and the meat cut up, we couldn't smell gas anymore, but we was real tired," he concluded.

"Did you leave the car parked at the barn last night?" Moon inquired.

"Yea, we was real tired, and we didn't want to wake Granny either," Lesiel admitted.

"The reason you still have gas this morning is because you backed up to the barn and there's a steep little hill that the barn sets on. The trunk and tank were tilted up! How high was the lowest hole, Bear?" the big man inquired.

"Oh, I'd say about six inches," Bear answered.

"Well, the gas tank mystery no longer will clutter the annals of unsolved mysteries, Moon Milligan to the rescue!"

"Lesiel, Hubert, in the office," Moon bellowed as he herded them toward the station door. He glanced at Bear and winked as he marched the gunmen into Sheriff Moon's office for sentencing."

"Boys, I'm going to tell you how it's going to be—" Moon started.

"Gonna fire us. Gonna fire us, ain't ya, Moon? Ain't ya?" Lesiel asked in anticipation.

"Shut up, Lesiel!" Hubert nervously shouted.

"You shut up!" Lesiel answered.

"Both you be quiet! If either of you Davie Crockett's kill, wound, shout at, or spit on a living thing out of season in a car, truck, tricycle, or moving train, I'll fire you! Then, I'll call Granny, the game warden, and the sheriff, and we'll all run you out of town! Do you understand me?"

Their heads were bobbing up and down faster than the little dog's head in the back of Barber Smith's car window.

You could see the relief in their faces. Moon thought,

If I could bring back the last time they angered me, I would. The car and truck together, it's not worth the loss of bond with these boys... men.

It was a typical cold, windy, and wet December Monday in Springo. Moon Milligan had a full schedule of parties to play. He had decided to cut his help back some at the station. Pump gas and sell cigarettes, cut the Brown boy's hours. Never far out of sight or mind, the dynamic duo came bouncing across the track and zoomed right into their favorite parking place. Making that traffic light was a big deal to Hubert. Moon was not disappointed as Lesiel walked in.

"Moon, did you see Hubert make that green light over in town?" Lesiel exhorted.

"Yea, he made it with time to spare," Moon teased.

"Hey, Moon, that Miss Tammy called us up at the house and wanted us to come down today and help her get ready for a party they're a havin' this Friday night. Can you get by without us? If 'en you can't, we'll tell her we can't come," a serious Hubert finished.

"Oh, I think that will be okay!"

"Well then, we better go, cause we want to stop down at Zeke Wilson's place and get some breakfast," Hubert said.

Lloyd's brother stopped by to tell Moon that Lloyd had the flu and wouldn't be around for a few days, but Mr. Vaughn said to tell him he was thinking about selling his 1948 Jeepster and he had just put a new top on it.

Around noon, Hubert and Lesiel pulled in to the station and sat talking for a few minutes before Hubert got out. Moon thought this was very unusual but realized that just when he had them figured out, they would surprise him.

"Hey, Hubert! You got done early. I thought you'd be there all day," Moon stated.

"We won't go back there again! Lesiel got us in big trouble, could a got us killed! That Mr. Johns' got guns all over that house. He's got three gun cases full, riffles, pistols, and everything. We can't ever go back!" Hubert declared.

Moon asked, "How did Lesiel get you into trouble?"

"Him and that Miss Tammy... they did! You see, when we got there, Mr. Johns was there, and he had us moving furniture around. Mr. Johns, he went to Dayton to pick up some flowers and other stuff Miss Tammy told him to get."

"Now when he left, she told me to start washing the front winders and watch for Mr. Johns to come back and to let her know when he was a comin' up the driveway. She was a fixin' something special for his Christmas, and she didn't want him to walk in and see it. She told me if I finished the winders to just sit there and look out and holler when I saw him a comin.' She took Lesiel in the back and said she had something for him to do. Well, I was a washin' them winders when I just had to go use the bathroom. So I went lookin' for it in a big hurry, cause I didn't want Mr. Johns to come home without me a seein' him. Well, I opened up the door to the bathroom, and it wasn't the bathroom! No-sir-e, it wasn't the bathroom! Lesiel and that woman was in bed, and neither of 'em had a single stitch of clothes on! They didn't even see me, they was so busy! I screamed as loud as I could, 'Lesiel, what do you think you're a doin' with that married woman? Daddy Frank will roll over in his grave ... God bless him and rest his soul.' He jumped up and ah ... started puttin' his clothes back on, and that Miss Tammy woman was just a laughin.' Shore'nuff, when we got to the front door, Mr. Johns was a getting' out of his car. We passed him on the way out. He asked us where we were going in such a hurry. I told him, 'We quit!' That Lesiel never said a word. He left it all on me! Said he was hungry and he wanted me to go into Dayton and buy some Kentucky chicken. I ain't takin' him anywhere! Moon, what am I goin' to do with him?" Hubert wanted to know.

Moon started to answer, "Just take him home, and you come on back, I'll—"

Hubert interrupted, "We didn't even get paid, and I didn't do nothing wrong. I want my pay. Lesiel got what he wanted."

"Hubert, listen to me. Things we do affect people around us—friends, strangers, and yes, family. That goes for good and bad. That's a lesson for all of us. Now take him home and come back ... and, Hubert, I'll see that *you* get *your* money," Moon finished.

As Hubert stormed out, Moon thought to himself, "After I get through playing the holiday parties, I'll put a stop to all the games people are playing!"

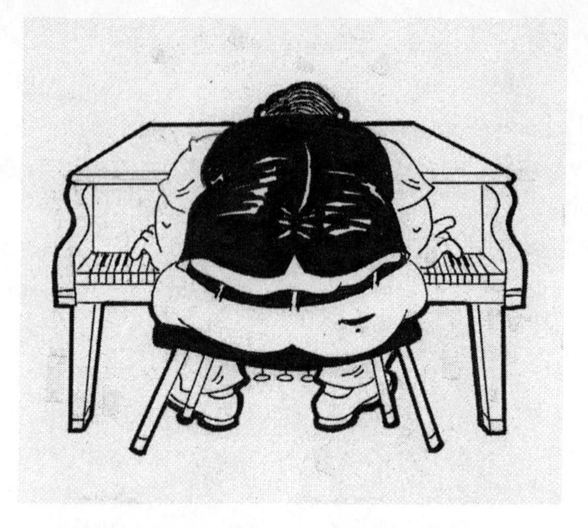

Count Down, Delay

The days slid by so quickly, Moon checked his calendar daily to make sure he was on schedule with his musical and banking engagements, in addition to all the details of the big day. He kept a close check on his three gang members—Lloyd (the Digger), Hubert (Thunder Road Brown), and Lesiel (the … well, just ol' Lesiel).

Betty Jo was in the kitchen early on a cold January morning fixing a lunch for Moon out of leftover roast beef from supper the evening before. She checked the biscuits in the oven and turned down the burner under the full pound of sausage being readied for the big guy's breakfast. The morning quiet was broken by the ring of the telephone.

"Hello," Betty Jo answered.

"I need to talk to Moon. It's Granny. She's sick, real sick. Lesiel's gone with the car, and I ain't got no truck keys. She's real bad, Miss Milligan, real bad. She's gonna die if'in I can't get her to the hospital. Tell Moon! Bye." The phone was hung up.

"Moon! Moon!" Betty Jo screamed.

Moon appeared in the doorway drying himself with a towel. He had just stepped out of the shower.

"What's wrong? Is it your daddy?"

"No, it's Granny! Hubert called, and she's real sick. Sounds bad. Do you want me to call the ambulance?"

"No, I can get there quicker, and who knows what's wrong," He answered as he quickly got dressed.

Betty Jo turned off the stove, grabbed her coat, and went out to start the Lincoln.

Moon jerked open the driver's side door. "Move over, I'm going to drive," he ordered.

"Moon Milligan, your hair is wet! You don't have on a T-shirt. You're going to catch your death of a cold!"

Moon zipped through ol' Springo without flashing lights or blaring siren. Why would he need either? Moon traveled faster than light or sound. With gravel flying through the air, the Lincoln came sliding to a stop in front of Granny's house. Hubert met the couple at the front door. Granny was on the couch. She was having trouble getting her breath. Moon grabbed her up, cradled her in his arms, and was out the door in but a moment.

Betty Jo sat in the spacious rear seat with Granny's head on her lap, as Granny moaned, not aware of her surroundings.

"She's burning up with fever, and her chest is really rattling," Betty reported.

As Moon pulled into the emergency entrance at Rhea County Hospital, he told Hubert to go in and tell them to come out and get Granny. Hubert was too distraught to answer but nodded his head before springing from the car and running the short distance to the hospital's entrance.

Betty Jo accompanied the attendants as they rolled Granny to the emergency room. Moon parked the car and then joined the others as the doctor started to check Granny out. He turned and asked Hubert and Moon to step out to the waiting room but asked Betty Jo to stay.

Moon remembered that it was time to open the gas station. He looked up Carl's phone number and was in luck. He told Carl to get his spare key ring from Bear and that he would be back as soon as he found out Granny's condition.

Moon and Hubert went out to the main waiting room. Bill Thedford's mother was the gray lady on duty that day. She had been a volunteer for years. Moon had a flashback. He remembered she had been a Red Cross volunteer back when he would wait for her and Bill to get to church. He always felt guilty around her and wondered, but never asked, if she knew he used her as an alibi.

"Hey, Moon, how are you? It's been a long time! Do you have someone in the hospital?" she inquired.

"Yes, you know Granny, Hubert and Lesiel's grandmother. Betty Jo and I brought her down. She seems pretty sick."

"I've seen her at the station a few times, but I really never met her. Of course everyone that gets gas from you know those boys. Is she related to your wife?" Mrs. Thedford asked. "Oh, by the way, Bill's moving back to Springo. He's buying the old Kelly Evans Grocery Store."

"I didn't know he had any grocery store experience?"

"Well, he doesn't, he's going to turn it into a seven-day convenience store operation."

"Well, that's great news but... man, I won't have an excuse to go to the Rio Vista for catfish now," Moon complained. "I sure did enjoy going down to Georgia."

As he looked to his right, he saw Hubert with his face in his hands. He had forgotten all about the boy's worry and pain for his grandmother.

"It was sure good seeing you, Mrs. Thedford, and tell Bill I'll be seeing him around," Moon replied as he quickly walked over to Hubert.

"Please let me know what I can do to help Granny. I'll be checking in on her," Mrs. Thedford lovingly answered.

"It's going to be alright, Hubert. They will take care of her here," the big guy reassured as he wedged into the seat beside the boy.

Soon, Betty Jo came out and gave a report on Granny's condition. Seems she had pneumonia, had a high fever, and they were waiting for her X-ray results. The doctor had decided to keep her a couple of days at least. Betty Jo told Moon that Hubert could go on back to see Granny but Moon needed to take him on home after that.

"I'm going to stay with her, Moon. You go on, and I'll call you and tell you what to bring me. I'll stay with her tonight if the doctor thinks it's necessary."

When this quiet little lady spoke directly to Moon in this matter-of-fact way, the big guy followed her marching orders. His Mama didn't raise no fool!

As Hubert and Moon got back to the car, Moon pointed his Lincoln north, and up Highway 27 they went. Moon had a burning question, he waited until they had traveled a few miles and then, "Hubert, where is Lesiel?" Moon inquired.

"He didn't come home last night. He went out with

some woman from Grandview last night. Leiseil was supposed to drive the truck, but I looked out and he was goin' up the road in the car. He left me with nothing to drive, 'cause he took the keys to the truck. All he wants to do is drink and run the roads," Hubert complained.

"Well, he's not carrying his share of the load around here. When we get back to town, you slip out the guns you boys have and bring them to me. You get the keys from Lesiel and come out to my house. I'll call some good ol' boys from Meigs County and they'll pay little brother a visit," Moon instructed.

"They the Klan, Moon, they the Klan! I don't want Lesiel hurt or run out of town like they did that Rupert Plemons a while back," Hubert exclaimed as his voice got louder and he began to tear up. "He did things to his girlfriend's little girl, and Lesiel ain't done nothing like that! He just drinks and spends our money running the roads and chasing them loose women!"

"Hubert! You just do like I tell you. When they come, you just go to the barn. He needs his butt whipped. His hide will grow back. If we don't stop his goings on now, he will get in serious trouble before we know it."

"Moon, you goin' to church over to that Baptist Church of Preacher Bookers?"

"Yea, not as often as I should," Moon answered.

"Could I go with you in the morning?"

"Sure, Hubert, I'll pick you up at ten thirty, and after church, we'll go down and visit Granny," Moon related as he pulled up to let Hubert out at home. "Oh, Hubert, Lesiel may want to come with you after tonight. Remember, just walk across the street to the barn!" Moon instructed. As Moon turned around, he noticed that the Chevy was back at home.

As Moon crossed the tracks, he looked over toward the station and smiled. Carl was pumping gas for Mr. Wasson, Bear was pumping gas into Hugh Perry's car, and Lloyd was cleaning the windshields.

Wow, Moon thought. *I need to leave more often.* As he exited his car, he found out the real concerns of his friends. They peppered him quickly with questions.

"How's Granny?" Bear gruffly asked.

"You didn't leave her by herself down there, did you?" Lloyd snapped.

"Thought I couldn't handle it, didn't you, Moon? I called in the A-team," a smiling Carl stated. "All kidding aside, I couldn't find the switch to turn on the pumps."

"That's okay, Carl. Never thought to show you how to open or close." Moon continued. "Granny's got pneumonia. Betty Jo is going to spend the night at the hospital with her. She's probably dehydrated also," he ended.

Moon asked Carl to stay to help. Bear disappeared around the corner of the building, much like he had after each visit. Lloyd hung around, and Moon could tell he had something on his mind. As soon as Carl went to wait on a customer, Lloyd unloaded.

"Deputy Morgan was down at the funeral home to make arrangements for traffic for the Roberts Funeral up at Roddy, and he came to the garage to talk to me. He said he didn't know you. He thought that Lesiel was kin to you. I straightened that out real quick."

"Well, what did Lesiel and me have to do with anything?" Moon angrily questioned.

"I'm trying to tell you, Moon, just get off your high horse, okay? Now, seems he was out on Grandview and Lesiel had run off the road about 2:00 a.m. Friday night, he got stuck in the mud. He was driving the '55 Chevy and had a woman with him, old enough to be his mother. Both were pretty drunk, and this Waldow, Shirley, I think he said, got real smart with him. He was getting ready to cuff her when a friend of this Shirley's came by and got the car out of the ditch. Deputy Morgan got this neighbor man to drive Lesiel back to her house in the Chevy. Well, Lesiel got real mouthy with the deputy and threatened to whip him, so Morgan said he walked back to the patrol car to call for backup. An older man drove up with two young guys. He said he would get Lesiel to go with them and not let him get behind the wheel," Lloyd finished.

"Lesiel's out of control," Moon stated. "I'm going to make a call and hopefully beat some sense into him. Go out front and keep Carl out of here, I've got to make a phone call. Tell you all about it in a few minutes."

"Yea, remind me to give you an update on our friend, the banker, when you get a chance," Lloyd stated as he walked out the front.

Moon picked up the phone and dialed Eddie Lee Jones's Demolition Service, better known as Eddie's Bar.

After four rings..."What?"

"Hey, Eddie Lee. You been dancing with your ex-wife's mother lately?" Moon asked.

"Moon! Where the hell you been, big man? Come on over, and let's party!" Eddie exclaimed.

"Don't do that a lot anymore. Need a favor," Moon responded.

For the next forty-five minutes, Moon explained his problems with Lesiel and how he wanted them to take care of it without any serious damage to the young Lesiel. Eddie Lee owed Moon for past favors at his bar. You see, Moon got his father-in-law to talk to the Meigs County Sheriff, keeping Eddie Lee out of jail. The demolition service name on his bar referred to humans, not automobiles! As he ended their conversation, Moon once again reminded Eddie Lee that this wasn't a *total* demolition, only a foundation shaking.

The third time Lloyd stuck his head in the door, Moon motioned for him to come on in as he hung up the phone.

"Sorry, Lloyd. Took a little longer to get the details straight. Now, what did you want to tell me?" Moon asked.

"Deputy Morgan gave me a little more information," Lloyd started.

"Oh, well just tell me what else Lesiel has done. I won't be surprised at anything," Moon answered.

"It doesn't involve Lesiel, it's about Hawthorn. Morgan said he pulled Hawthorn over for speeding on Roddy Straight and wrote him a ticket for going seventy miles per hour in a fifty-five," Lloyd said.

"Great, it couldn't happen to a more deserving guy," Moon laughed.

"That's not all, Moon. Mrs. Hawthorn was in the car also, and she was crying and had a bruise on her cheek.

Morgan said her left wrist had a bandage on it. He asked her how she got them, and her eyes darted at Bob, then she looked down and said she had fallen," Lloyd stated.

"When are we going to get him? He's as sorry as they come! You need to stop worrying about Lesiel and get your gang friends to beat the hell out of Hawthorn, I'll even help, and you know I don't cotton to that bunch of crap from across the river," the sweating, red-faced, angry digger steamed.

Moon felt a chill. His feet were about to freeze. He still had on his good shoes. He hadn't had time to put on his insulated boots, and evening was fast approaching.

"Lloyd, close the door, buddy. I'm freezing," he ordered as he continued. "Hawthorn's got money, and he's got a lot of influence around here. He'll probably get that ticket fixed, even if the Sheriff doesn't like him. It's time to put our plan in place. If we can pull this off, he'll be under suspicion by the fed's and, at the very least, he'll be exposed along with that tramp, Tammy. I just bet ol' Mr. R.M. Johns III will get Hawthorn fired, and he'll be ruined in the banking business. Mr. Johns is big in the banking community of Chattanooga and Knoxville. He's what the big boys call a shaker and maker. I'll bet he'll be doing more shaking than making," the big man concluded with a grin and then a thundering, belly-shaking laugh!

A grin came to Lloyd's face, "Let's do it, Moon!"

Using his newfound resource, Moon left early. Leaving Carl in charge of closing, he was free to proceed with chores at hand—talking to Betty Jo without the interruptions of the station.

Moon dialed up Betty, and she reported that Granny's fever was down and she was breathing better but was not out of the woods just yet.

He changed clothes and gathered the items that Betty had asked for and headed south. Moon didn't want to be around when Eddie Lee and his boys paid Lesiel a social call. It was strange; he could trust Eddie more than his own banker. Kind of like the boys on the city garbage truck, no one wanted details of their daily work but it was needed to keep things in order.

Moon pulled off the highway at the 27 Lounge (it was really a beer joint) to use the pay phone at the end of the building. He dialed up Granny's number, and Hubert answered.

"How's it going, Hubert?" Moon asked.

"Lesiel's gone back to bed. I think he's ah planning to go out later tonight," Hubert reported.

"Did you get the keys to both vehicles?"

"I got the ones to the Chevy and the truck. Moon, they ain't gonna hurt him bad are they?" Hubert pleaded.

"You don't want him to keep taken Granny's money and worrying her to death, do you? Just do as I say. I just hope he straightens up before somebody gets killed by his drunk driving, don't you?"

"Yea, do you think I could drive on down and see Granny, Moon?"

"Hubert, if that's what you want. Do you want to ride down with me? I'm using the pay phone at the 27 Lounge. I'll drive back to the station and pick you up there!"

"I'd like that. I don't know how to find her once I get there, Moon."

"See you in about ten minutes," Moon answered.

It was a wonderful time for Hubert and Granny. You could see the love in their eyes, and this man-boy was hurting so to see his Granny, the only mother he had ever known, hurting so. Moon slipped out of the room and quickly dried his eyes on this sleeve. As he re-entered the room, he saw the tear-reddened eyes of this loving young man, and as he turned toward Granny, he saw a smile, a smile of pure and wonderful joy. It was joy so pure just to be in Hubert's presence.

Betty Jo and Moon spent most of the evening in the waiting room talking. Eventually the conversation led to her asking about Lesiel. Moon did as any man in this position would do-he lied. How could he tell her about Lesiel's activities of the past days? He had taken care of everything. Didn't every man have the call to fix every problem that arose?

"No need to worry, Betty Jo."

The trip back to Springo was quiet. Moon tried several times to start a conversation with Hubert about most anything except what most burdened their thoughts. Moon pulled into the station to let Hubert out.

"Would you follow me home, Moon? I don't know what I'll find. I don't know what I'm s'pose to do if 'en they are still there and ah what if'en he's hurt real bad, I ah…"

"I'll be right behind you, Hubert," Moon assured him.

They pulled into the driveway. The house appeared to be dark, but as Moon got out of the Lincoln, he could see a light escaping from a rear window.

Hubert reached for the doorknob and started to step in, *bam,* he slammed into the locked door. The shaken and nervous young man fumbled for his keys.

"Calm down, Hubert."

Finally, the key slid into the lock, and the pair entered. Surprisingly, the living room was just at Hubert had left it, neat and everything in its place.

The light was spilling from the half-open door of the back bedroom. Cautiously, the pair approached the door, and Hubert pushed it open. The sight they saw was shocking.

Parts of what used to be a chair were scattered about, a small chest of drawers was overturned, and there laid Lesiel, stretched across the bed. Moon flipped on the overhead light. Lesiel was looking at the pair, and as he tried to roll over to his back, he let out a yelp. He remained on his stomach, grimacing with pain. His white T-shirt was torn and streaked with blood. One of his pant legs was hiked up to his knee, exposing red welts.

"Oh, Lesiel, are you gonna die?" a distraught brother cried.

"Who did this, boy? Do you know?"

"Moon, I ain't never seen 'em before. Honest... they said they'd come back if I ever—"

"If you ever what, Lesiel? If you ever what? Do you know what you did?" Moon asked.

"Yea, they was ah four of 'em. They had straps. I won't ever do nothing again. I'll work an ah give money back to Granny. Oh, I hurt! Is Granny gonna be okay, Moon? Don't let 'em hurt me again. Don't, Moon... please! Oh! Oh!" Lesiel moaned.

"Hubert, go see if you can find some iodine and some of Granny's salve."

Moon returned from Granny's house around nine thirty with a better feeling about Granny's condition. It had been a long time since he had been home alone. His mind constantly in drive, he thought, *I'll just take this opportunity to write Miss Tammy a reminder.*

Dear Tammy,

On behalf of the Lawson brothers, I wish to call your attention to your lack of payment to Hubert for his work, and especially Lesiel, for his personal services preformed. Lack of payment shall force further legal pursuit; including the notification of the Honorable R.M. Johns III. Please send cash or check payable to:

Hubert Lawson
C/O Springo Shell Service Station
Highway 27, Springo, Tennessee

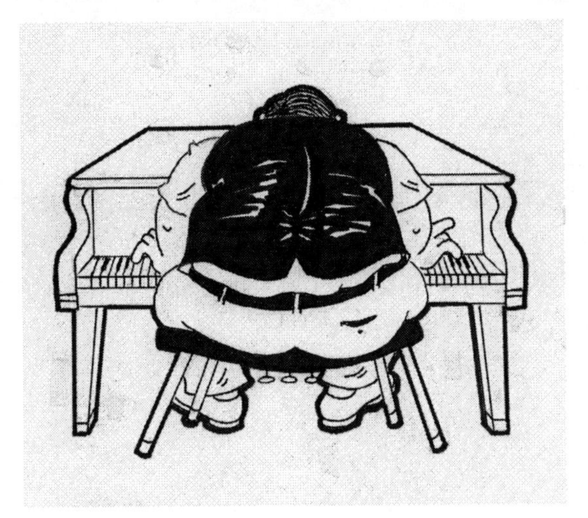

Count Down, Restart

Granny had recovered and returned home. Lesiel had healed and appeared to have changed his ways. Hubert, good, steady Hubert, was happy because his family of Granny and Lesiel were happy.

Hubert had been attending Preacher Booker's church but hadn't been able to persuade brother Lesiel to go. He told Moon that he was a working on it.

Business at the Shell station had never been better. Moon hired Lloyd's nephew, Carl, fulltime, and Hubert and Lesiel worked most days without a schedule.

Moon loved playing all the December parties, but he was happy to welcome the New Year. He had some unfinished business to attend to.

With a full crew at work, he had the time to get his chair leaning with just the right tilt. His eyelids were quickly adjusting to their proper angle, closed, as the auxiliary heater hummed a rhythmic tone.

"Hey, Moon, let's rob a bank!"

Down with the chair, up with the lids, to view the

smiling face of the ugly gravedigger from a distance of exactly six inches.

"If I had a gun," the big guy said through clenched teeth.

"Moon, Moon. You're sleeping your life away! Look around you. Two cars on the front, Carl's got 'em both a filling. Lesiel's putting on a set of new tires, and Hubert's greasing and changing oil, and best of all, it's raining for the umpteenth time in the last week, but your best friend is here a lookin' at you."

"Ex-best friend," Moon growled.

"Seriously, Moon, what's the schedule on *the plan?*"

"I think it's time. Let's look at a week from tomorrow," Moon answered.

"Wake up, Moon, today is Thursday, we're still planning on a Thursday, aren't we?"

"Oh yea, lost a day somewhere. A week from today!" Moon corrected.

"I need to let Carl off. He's too sharp. He might pick up on something. But what reason can I give him? Don't want to make him mad and loose him," Moon worried.

"No problem! When he comes back in, I'll tell him I need him at the cemetery, and you can tell him everything is okay with you. I'll pick him up early next Thursday when I get finished putting the ball cap on top of the Five and Ten Store. He can leave his car here, and when we get through with business, I'll bring him back here. You said everything needs to look normal that day. So we'll all be where we are on every other work day when the job goes down," Lloyd finished with surprising confidence.

The next six days, not a word was said of *the job,* it was set. The plan was set . . . so simple, so, so, well, so *final.*

Betty Jo finished with her Saturday morning trip to Shipley's Supermarket, paid her bills, and picked up the day's mail from the post office and then stopped by the station.

"Moon, here's the station's mail, and this looks personal."

She handed him the stack of mail. On top was a hand written letter with no return name or address. It had a Dayton postmark stamp. He opened it as Betty Jo watched out of the corner of her eye while trying to look uninterested.

Moon pulled out a check for $100.00 signed by Tammy Johns. He gave it to Jo.

"Why, this is made out to Hubert and Lesiel Lawson. I guess it's for back pay," Moon said as Jo handed it back to him.

"Moon, I was talking to Susanne about going to Crossville next Thursday, since Bob's always in Dayton. Thought we would leave when you come to open up. Would that work out with you?"

"Next Thursday... ah its just another day. Think that would be just fine for you ladies to be out of town. Now, you could pick-up something special for me for supper."

"You're always thinking about eating. Well, I'll bring you back something special."

Thursday morning was identical to the previous five days—pouring rain. It was too wet for Carl to do anything at the cemetery, but Lloyd was on top of the potential problem. He had made arrangements with Mr.

Vaughn for Carl to work building storage shelves at the funeral home.

Lloyd was waiting as Moon came in, just like he had done so many times.

"Hey, Moon, guess what?"

"What?"

"Come here and look. Did you know you can see the hat I put on top of Phillip's Five and Ten last night?"

"Well, I'll be! Good job, Lloyd. I looked from inside the bank a while back, and you have to really look to see the top of the ledge of the Five and Ten. Have you looked to see if the garbage can you placed at the back of the bank last night is still there?"

"Ten-four, good buddy. Calm down, everything's in place, big man."

"Oh, my gosh!" Moon exclaimed, looking out the window. "What's going on? The boys are driving their Chevy. They need the truck to haul the loot."

Lesiel pulled up in front of the door.

"Moon! Moon! I need the jumper cables. Left the lights on when I got home last night, I had to go to the store and get Granny…"

"Hubert, get the jumper cables and get on back. I need you to get the truck down here!"

"Okay, Moon, we haven't forgot about the trick this morning."

Across the tracks, at the Bank of Springo, Mr. Hawthorn walked in promptly at 8:20 a.m. that wet, chilly January,

Thursday morning. As usual, he moved directly toward his office. He paused to speak only to Mrs. Thompson and then proceeded into his office. He slid into his over-stuffed, leather chair while reaching for the telephone. His fingers dialed each number as he impatiently waited for the dial to return before proceeding to the next.

Completing his task, he sat back in his chair, paused a moment, and then began talking into the telephone in a quiet tone. As he completed his conversation, he reached into his desk drawer and retrieved a pack of Rolaids.

Mrs. Thompson stepped to his office door as he popped a couple of Rolaids into his mouth.

"Heartburn again, Mr. Hawthorn?"

"Indigestion, indigestion. Every time I stop and get sausage and biscuits, it's indigestion time. Boy I love my sausage and biscuits. Becky, it's Thursday, pouring rain, and I've got to go to the meeting. The meeting! If any-thing ever came up of importance, they could just call me. I don't think Springo First will merge or open a branch in Dayton. They sure don't need my okay, one way or the other. I'm happy living in Springo, and I don't care to move to Dayton. However, if I don't attend and set there and smile, I won't be living in Springo," he concluded.

"Mr. Hawthorn, I'll take care of everything here. It's going to be the usual Thursday . . . slow, slow, slow. You be careful of water over the road. Hope Piney Creek doesn't get out of her banks," she worried.

Hawthorn pulled into the Shell station at nine thirty sharp. Moon stepped further back into the shadows of the grease rack.

As instructed, Hubert went out to pump the banker's gas.

"Hi, Hubert, where's Moon this morning?"

"He's working on the books, Mr. Hawthorn," Hubert lied.

"Fill 'er up and wipe off my headlights, they've got a lot of road film on them, Hubert."

"Six fifty, Mr. Hawthorn. Got them headlights cleaned. You gonna need that passenger wiper changed pretty soon. It's beginning to come apart. It's one of them long ones. I'll tell Moon, and he can a look it up. You see, he's got this big, thick book, tells him what size your car—"

"Here's seven bucks, Hubert, keep the change. I don't have time to listen to you babble," Hawthorn snapped as he closed his window and hurriedly pulled out.

A horn blared, and a car swerved to barely avoid a head-on collision as the banker headed south for his *special* meeting.

"Mr. Bob shure is in a big hurry for his big meeting," Hubert related.

"Yea, I bet he is," Moon scorned. "Hubert, get in your truck. Go to the dime store and get me a pack of number two pencils. Now when you come out, look to the back of the bank and make sure the new garbage can is still there. Got it?"

"Come on, Moon, who are you going to play the trick on? Tell me... tell me!"

"Shut up, Hubert. If you say one more word, I won't tell you anything. I'll get someone else to help out. Now, can I trust you to keep your mouth shut for a couple of weeks?"

Moon moved close to Hubert; the veins in his neck were standing out, and his face was bright red with anger.

"No, no, no, I won't breathe a word to anyone, not even Lesiel. Okay, okay. I'm sorry, Moon. I didn't mean to get you mad. I'm sorry. You're the best friend I got!"

Moon turned and started to his office at the rear of the grease rack. Lesiel followed the big man to the office door.

"Where'd Hubert go, Moon?"

"He went to the store for me. Now get back to washing Doc Ransom's car. Get the inside windows clean too, just use a little rubbing alcohol on your cloth, it's setting in the window."

"Be a lot better if'en he didn't smoke them big ole cigars all the time, makes them windows streak," Lesiel complained.

"Doc gets his car detailed at Jimmy Galloway's next to the Double-Q most of the time."

"There ain't no gas station next to the Double-Q," Lesiel fired back.

"Jimmy been cleaning up cars since before you were born. He works at TVA and does the cleanups, evenings and Saturdays. Shut up and clean the windows. The car wouldn't be here now if Jimmy was off work. You better understand. If I don't have work, you won't have any money."

Moon exhaled deeply. For some reason, he was uptight this morning, must be the weather. One thing for sure, Doc Ransom and his family were fine folks. Doc had been stopping in more often since he retired as the towns only dentist. It was nearly two years before Doc Leonard started his practice.

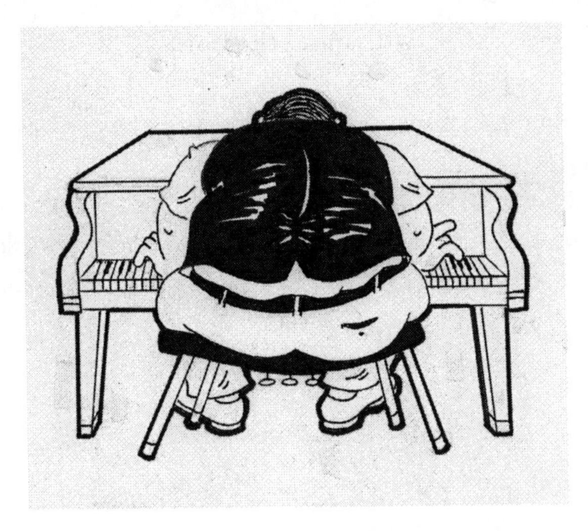

Cold Feet or Wet Feet

Moon slammed the door, flipped on the light, and went directly to a pile of rags. He pulled out a third, two-way radio he had borrowed from the Springo Fire and Rescue. Moon opened the door part way and called for Lesiel to take care of the front. He closed the door and plopped down in his large, overstuffed yard sale chair. He was already tired; nerves that had lay dormant for years became front line soldiers. His thoughts began to retreat into the dangerous territory of self-doubt. Moon's blundering, stumbling forward, never resulted in the first sign of weakness. His inner code of subconscious stability was based on years of a just-do-it, smooth-it-out-later attitude. Today was different though; he was rehashing every detail in his mind.

Hubert and Lesiel had been told sketchy details of an elaborate trick he was going to play on a friend and that their help was needed. Their orders were: "You must not say a word to anyone... ever! Don't talk about it to each other, even Granny. When it's over in a week or two, I'll tell you all about it."

Suddenly, his thoughts were completely immersed in self-doubt. He questioned himself. How, even in weeks or months ahead, could he give them a story they would not repeat?

Lloyd slowly opened the door.

"Moon, I need the radio now. I'm going to stay down at the cemetery. It's pouring rain, coming down in sheets. I'll be in the truck to stay dry. Will this weather affect these two-ways, Moon?"

"Nope, unless lightning strikes you while you're using it," Moon joked, slightly returning to a Moon of confidence.

There followed a long silence with Lloyd staring at the radio, as if it were the source of his demise.

"Lighten up, ol' friend, you won't be struck with or without the radio. Your truck cab's the safest place you could be." Moon continued, "It's January, cold, pouring rain; there won't be much, if any, lightning!"

Lloyd picked up an old gunnysack and carefully wrapped it around the radio. He and Moon walked slowly to the front of the lube bay. They stood and surveyed the scene. Sheets of water cascaded down, a car slowly heading north, plowing through as if fording a river.

Suddenly, a flash followed by a *bam, bam* shook the station, and the deluge intensified beyond any level Moon could remember.

"Moon, it's not too late to cancel the whole thing," the good friend stated.

"Your boots must be leaking, that's why you are getting wet feet," chided Moon. "You're going to be across the street from the bank. You will not see any money. You're not going to touch any money. Every gun you own is under lock and key at your house. You're not going to break any laws. You're going to drive up Rhea Avenue, following a couple of friends from a distance, and turn north onto Highway 68. Then, you will turn right onto Sandtown Road, drive right on by as the boys stop at Granny's barn. You will drive back to the Shell station and eat lunch with me, as you have hundreds of times. Don't forget the mayo, we're out," the big man concluded as his lack of breath suddenly demanded his silence.

The radio check had gone off without a hitch. Lesiel's handle was Roger. He had gotten real confused when to say Roger or "Roger, Roger" and "over and out." The instructions were simple. If Moon said, "Come in, Roger," Lesiel was to answer, "Hello," and when Moon said, "Over and out," Lesiel would use a special word that had never ever before been used to end a radio message, "Bye."

If the military had used an elaborate code such as this during World War II, they could have left the Indians on their reservations.

Hubert's job was to drive the truck, and the only handle he needed would be to control Lesiel.

Lloyd's handle was Planter; he was always planting someone at Springo's Cemetery.

Moon's was Skinny; it was still a big kid's game in the back of Moon's mind. Everything was surreal; the whole plan wouldn't be this close to going down if not for a friend's betrayal.

Bob Hawthorn's treatment of his wife, both emotionally and physically, had infuriated Moon. Susanne was a friend, a lady, and a wonderful woman. She lived for her husband and supported his endeavors, always.

"Yes, I bet he was in a hurry this morning... a real loving hurry. Have a nice day, Bob!"

Lloyd had sensed Moon's mental distance, so the grave-digger had taken the opportunity to pull his coat over his head and slip out to his truck. The heavy rain let up as he turned to drive up the hill to the cemetery. As he pulled into his favorite parking spot, he could see the traffic on Highway 27 with their headlights reflecting off the standing water. He turned to his right but couldn't see the mountain that had given him peace so many times, because the fog had completely encapsulated it. He thought of the many times the view had soothed his troubled mind. Few people could appreciate the beauty of a January view of a barren mountainside stripped of the buds of spring or the misty, summer morning's invitation to the lush, fully-adorned green vastness. People would travel great distances to see the fall foliage, rich with color from God's un-tethered paintbrush.

This morning, hidden by weather, his mind could still see the rocks and cliffs, visible only when the trees were stripped bare of their seasonal foliage. Peace, peace for all seasons, provided not by man or a single sound, but by God's creation.

Startled by the arrival of a single hickory nut dropping a few feet onto the hood of his truck, his escape from reality abruptly ended. He looked down and uncovered his radio.

Reality

"You boys pay attention now. I want you two to watch the front. I've got to make a phone call, and I don't want to be bothered," Moon ordered as he walked back to the office.

"Hello, Miss Becky. Moon Milligan here. Could I speak to Bob, please?"

"He's gone to his Thursday meeting."

"Oh gee, I forgot what day it is," he lied. "Could you have him call me as soon as he gets back, please?"

"Sure, but it will be two at the earliest, Moon. Could I possibly help you?" Becky asked.

"No, I wanted to talk to him about a non-banking matter."

"Well, I'll give him the message. Have a good day," the always-cheerful Becky ended.

Moon turned and called for the boys, and they promptly responded, grinning from ear to ear.

"Is it time, Moon? Is it time?"

"Yes, it's time. Go to the storage room and get the radio off my desk."

As Lesiel whirled and started to the back, Moon said, "Listen, listen. Get a gunny sack from the corner and keep it covered up until you need it."

"Hubert, remember. You're to drive. Leave here and drive up 68 to Norris's Car Lot. Drive like you're out for a Sunday cruise. Turn around and drive back down Jackson and just drive around town until I radio you. Don't cross to this side of the tracks, just drive anywhere but Front Street. When I radio you, go directly to the back of the bank. Lesiel is to load the shiny, new garbage can that is there. Lay it down in the truck bed and cover it with the old tarp. Drive away on up Jackson, not too slow. Don't drive fast enough to blow the tarp off. Take it to Granny's barn and hide it where we fixed the place. Cover it with the tarp, and then bust open a bale of that hay and cover it. Come straight back here, not a word to anybody. You can eat lunch with me and Lloyd. We'll not say a word about the trick to each other or anyone else, okay?"

"Okay, Moon."

Moon picked up his radio and ordered the planter to move into position at the observation point across from the bank.

"Okay, boys, hit the road. Keep on the move until I radio you to move in," Moon ordered.

As the pair started out the door, Moon exclaimed, "Wait! We need to do a radio check. Make sure it's on and I'll call as you start up 68."

"Okay, good buddy," Lesiel affirmed.

As Hubert drove off, Moon remembered an important detail. He reached in a cabinet and took out two out-of-gas signs and hurriedly took them to the pump island and returning to the station, turned out the lights, and locked the front door.

"Skinny, come in, Skinny."

"Go ahead, Digger ,Planter."

"In position, over and out."

"Come in, Roger."

"Hey, Skinny, ah ... ah ... go ahead, Skinny."

"You're loud and clear, Roger, over and out."

"Bye."

Moon was sweating profusely. The boys could cause that even in normal times.

Why, oh why had he let Lesiel be the radio man? Moon thought as he sat and waited.

A customer pulled up to the pumps and sat there.

"Well, I don't know who that is. Guess he can't read. I'll just sit here and not move. Oh, he's seen the sign. Whew! He's leaving." Moon took a deep breath and dialed the Springo Bank. A small transistor radio was setting next to the phone. Moon had carefully turned the dial off station and turned up the volume until it reached a moderate hum, mixed with intermittent crackle.

"Good morning, Springo Bank. How may I help you?" a very familiar voice asked.

"Listen carefully," he began to talk in a sub-low voice disguised by the crackle of the radio and a piece of hard candy the big man had placed between his upper and lower jaw teeth. "We have Bob Hawthorn. As I speak to you, Thompson, I have a gun stuck in his mouth."

"Let me talk to him! This is not funny!" Mrs. Thompson ordered.

"Shut up! If you don't cooperate, the next sound you hear will be a .38 revolver going off, blowing your boss's brains out! You are being watched. Stand at your desk. Look straight across the lobby to the window. There is a sharp shooter in place on the roof of the dime store. Do not give any signs, push any alarms, or act in any way to draw suspicion. Sit down, Thompson. Trust me, the bank has been rigged with six sticks of dynamite. The man at the depot across the street is set. It's up to you—blow or no blow. Now, Thompson, do you still need to talk to your boss, or am I the boss, it's up to you?"

"What do you want me to do?" she asked in a shaky voice.

"Call that young male teller to your desk and take him into the boss's office in sixty seconds or less. Bring him up-to-date. Hand the phone to him. Remember, if you try to talk or relate to anyone else in the bank, Mr. Hawthorn will have a permanent headache. Now, lay the phone down, walk into Hawthorn's office, pick the phone up, push the button, go back to your desk, and hang up. Got it?"

"Yes."

"Now, get the kid into the office ... *now!*"

The next twenty seconds seemed to last long enough to fill up a Mercury Turnpike Cruiser. Suddenly, he heard Becky's voice again, without a hitch, almost word for word. She went through the instructions. As Moon listened, a shaky young man came on.

"This is Jim Bates."

"Bates, do you understand?"

"Well, I can hear you pretty good!"

Moon suddenly sees the humor, then, just as quickly, after adjusting his speech deflector, he resumed.

"Do you understand that I have a gun halfway down Hawthorn's throat?"

"Yes, sir."

"Now, I'm going to give the instructions to what's-her-name, ah... ah."

"You mean Miss Becky, sir?"

"Yea, if you're talking about Thompson. Give her the phone, *now!*"

Bang! Rattle!

"Sorry, he dropped the phone, Mr... what should I call you?" Mrs. Thompson inquired.

"It depends. Tom, Dick, or Harry, and if you don't do quickly what I say, call me murderer!"

"Yes, sir. What do you want me to do?" she asked.

"Lay down the phone, but don't hang it up under any circumstances. I want you and the Bates boy to go open the vault and take every bill out, starting with the tens, and don't forget the bundles of thousands."

Just a wild guess as Moon began to loosen up; it was kind of like play-acting.

"Place the bundles in the empty typing paper boxes. Make sure there's at least $100,000. If not, get the big bills out of the teller trays. Got that?"

"Okay," Mrs. Thompson reluctantly answered.

"Now, while Jim Bob Bates boy is carrying them out the side door, you go back into the lobby and talk to the tellers. Everything is normal. Be calm. Remember, the phone is still open. Go back to the phone, and when Bates is finished, have him come into the office again.

"Now, let me talk to Bates!"

"Hello, sir, Jim Bates here."

"Jim, your job is to go with Thompson and carry

the boxes out the side door and to the back of the bank. Beside the trash dumpster is a bright, shiny, new trash-can. Dump the money in it and put the empty boxes on top of the dumpster. Now listen, if it won't all go into the new can, just set the full boxes beside it. Got that?"

"Yes, sir."

"Are you sure?"

"Yes."

"When you finish, don't look around. Go directly to Hawthorn's office. Don't hang up the phone. Just lay it down. If you see a strange package wrapped with red tape, don't touch it, whatever you do, *don't touch it,* now go!"

Clunk, the sound of the phone being laid down.

The next minutes seemed to last ten thousand seconds. The first minute he spent making a muffler out of an ol' foam cushion and tape, to slip the bottom of the phone into, just in case someone tried to hear background noise at his station. Finally, the silence was broken, and Moon nearly jumped out of his skin.

"Skinny, come in, Skinny!"

"The *mail* is in the box. Two on the ground. That's a total of six, over!"

"Good job, Planter. Will contact delivery, over and out."

"Calling, Roger … Calling, Roger. Come in, Roger. This is Skinny. Come in, Roger."

"Hey, Skinny! Roger here."

"Pick up time, Roger."

"What, moo … ah, Skinny. What?"

"Pick up the can and the two boxes, Roger!"

"Okay, okay, gotcha."

Moon heard a weak sound from his telephone and grabbed it out of its foam insulator.

"Hello, hello, let me speak to Mr. Hawthorn," a nervous voice spoke.

"Hey, the rules haven't changed. Bates placed four boxes in the can and sat two beside it, true?"

Muffled voice talking. "Yes, he said that's exactly what he did. Can I please talk to Bob?" she asked.

"Oh, now it's Bob? Well, check your watch. In exactly thirty minutes, if our men watching every move inside and out of the bank see it's clear, Bobby will be released. You really need to re-key the lock on the door leading to the conference room upstairs. I'll tell Bobby to hurry back to the bank, since there wasn't a meeting today. Come to think of it, has there ever been a meeting on Thursday in Dayton with Mr. Robinson? I suggest you call him about thirty minutes from now. By the way, if the Bank of Springo ever needs a new president, you would get my vote all the way from Miami.

"These are your final instructions. Check the Dime Store roof; you still have company. Leave the phone as it is. When the time is up, I suggest you call your local police, and just because you have been a good girl, here's your tip: the honorable president of the Bank of Springo has been detained at the home of Tammy and R.M. Johns III. I'll bet the Honorable Sheriff McCoy will know the address. Good day, Mrs. Thompson."

As Moon placed the phone back in the custom case, he heard the crackle of the radio being keyed.

"Planter calling Skinny. Come in, Skinny."

"Go ahead, Planter. This is Skinny."

"Delivery secured and in transport on public road, over."

"Follow up, Planter. Over and out."

Moon sat back in his chair and exhaled. He felt as though this was the twenty-fifth hour of a twenty-four hour day! Boy, he felt good, as he thought about poor ol' Bob and how sore his mouth must be from the gun. He exploded into a deep belly laugh.

Lloyd was on his way back to town as he checked his watch. Perfect, he had ten minutes left on the thirty-minute restriction placed on the bank job by the master mind.

He turned and drove down Jackson Avenue, as he had for years, then, behind the Legion Hall and up to the backside of the Dime Store. Quickly, taking the end of a one hundred foot, nylon fishing line, he gave a hard jerk. Hand-over-hand, he retrieved his catch—a dirty, wet baseball cap right off the head of the invisible bank robber. As he pulled out and traveled down Front Street, he shook his head. Moon Milligan, what a mind! How had he put it all together? *He's so talented; I bet he could play a piano!*

As he entered the station, Moon was all smiles. Lloyd noticed that the phone was back in place and the big guy was Humming.

"Moon, are you going to leave the out-of-gas sign out all day?"

Nearly knocking the Digger down, Moon grabbed

the signs and looked around to see if anyone was watching. As he re-entered the station, he realized how wet he was.

"Lloyd, do you realize it hasn't slacked up all morning? I bet we've got six inches."

"What a great day to rob a bank, big guy. I hope ol' Bob appreciates all our hard work."

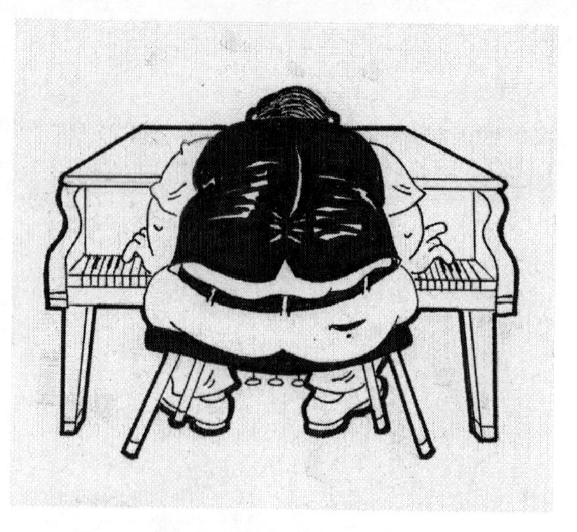

Picking Up the Pieces

Back at the bank, Mrs. Thompson was busy. She had the bank door locked and placed a call to Springo chief of police, Sam Charles; Rhea County sheriff, Mac McCoy's office; and, after a brief search, she found and called the TBI office in Knoxville, the bank robbery headquarters for East Tennessee. She was given the number of Agent Robert Stoker, since he could get there quickly from Chattanooga.

For the last thirty minutes or so, a thought had been running through her mind, *Where was Mr. Hawthorn?* She had so much respect for him. He was always a gentleman. This talk, after all, was from a bank robber. How did he know about those meetings? Mr. Hawthorn said only he and she herself from Springo Bank were to know of the meetings. Only Mr. Robinson and a couple of his trusted board members were aware of the branch plan.

Before she realized it, she was waiting as the phone rang at the Dayton Bank and Trust.

"Dayton Bank and Trust, this is Ann. How can I help you?"

"Ann, this is Becky at Springo Bank. Is Mr. Robinson in?"

"He was with a customer, let me ... see ... no, he's in. I'll buzz him."

"Hello, Becky. How's ol' Bob this morning?" Mr. Robinson asked.

Suddenly, she had a weak feeling come over her. "Do you not meet every Thursday with Mr. Hawthorn?" she asked.

"Wednesdays ... Wednesday afternoon. He must be golfing with someone else Becky," he said, laughing.

"I'm sorry for bothering you, Mr. Robinson. I must go."

"Tell Bob I said for him to bring a boat and we'll play this afternoon, if you can find him." He laughed.

Quickly, Becky tried to gain control of her emotions. She had no idea where Mr. Hawthorn was. She was in control of day-to-day operations if he was out of the bank, and by golly, she was in control.

Chief Charles and Patrolman Herb Jenkins arrived and were quickly briefed. As she went through the robbery step-by-step, she remembered the man on the roof. She and Chief Charles quickly backed over by her desk. The roofline was clean.

County Deputy Morgan tapped on the side door with his flashlight and was let in. Chief Charles asked Patrolman Jenkins and Deputy Morgan to secure the alley behind the bank with crime scene tape. Neither had rain gear on, so they went to plan B.

"Go to your patrol cars and put it on Deputy Morgan. I can't give you orders, that's the sheriff's responsibility."

"Chief, I've always worked with your people. It's not a problem. You're in charge until the sheriff gets here!"

The sheriff arrived and was in charge of maintaining security at the bank until the TBI arrived.

"Since we have no descriptions of the robbers, only a voice, no car, truck, or airplane, this one is for Bob Stoker, the TBI man, to figure out. He should be here any minute. I talked to him on the radio, and he's on his way."

"Sheriff, do you have any idea where Mr. Hawthorn might be? There wasn't a meeting in Dayton, and that's where he said he was going," Mrs. Thompson reported.

The color suddenly drained from the sheriff's face.

"No idea, I'll check a few things out when Agent Stoker gets here."

As Agent Stoker arrived, he was met by Sheriff McCoy. Becky noticed that the TBI man was trying to separate himself from McCoy.

Agent Stoker, a tall, neatly-dressed man, noticed Mrs. Thompson and left the Sheriff standing and walked over to talk with her.

"Mrs. Thompson, I'm Robert Stoker with the TBI out of the Chattanooga office. I've spoken with Agent Conner from Knoxville. He said that you had notified his office."

"Yes, I went by the procedure Mr. Hawthorn had given me if he wasn't here!"

"Let's step into the office and close the door. Now, tell me what you know about the whereabouts of Mr. Hawthorn?"

Becky proceeded to tell the agent each fact of the

morning, as they had occurred in a proper timeline. When she related the conversation with Mr. Robinson of Dayton Bank and Trust, Agent Stoker's head rose from his notepad, and in a hard stare, he asked, "Did you have any knowledge, hint, or suspicion about Mr. Hawthorn's character prior to this morning?"

"No, sir, not at all . . . never!" she firmly stated.

Stoker moved quickly to the door, opened it, and asked, "Sheriff, would you step in here, please?"

As the sheriff came into the office, Agent Stoker gruffly questioned, "Have you put out an APB on Mr. Hawthorn?"

"Ah, no, not yet."

"Well, you've been here going on an hour and the bank president's location is not known. Unless you know something I don't, Sheriff, he may be a hostage."

"No, I have some ideas, but I don't know anything for sure," the sheriff stammered.

"Mrs. Thompson, would you please step out and ask the chief to not let anyone in or out, except Agent Conner and his people? Thank you, and don't speak with anyone about the events of this morning, except an agent of the TBI. Thank you again."

At the Shell station, the crew was getting ready for a big celebration lunch. Moon sent Hubert to Shipley's to pick up the mayo and a couple of the biggest onions they had. Hubert came back all excited.

"They got the bank closed down today. That Nancy told me."

"Probably because of all the rain; everything is flooded," Moon said.

"Hope ol' Piney don't get too high and wash us away," Lesiel worried.

"The county went in there a couple years ago when she was so dry, cleaned it out good. Don't think it will be a problem," Lloyd assured.

A warm front had moved in, and the temperature had risen to sixty-four degrees on this wet, January day.

Moon tried to keep the boys busy, but it was a real task. There was no gas business. The weather had taken most of the traffic off the road. Front Street was deserted, except for an increasing amount of autos at the bank. *Wonder what could be going on?* As the boys were cleaning the lube rack with kerosene and brushes, Moon and Lloyd were beginning to work on *Plan B.*

"Here's the plan, Lloyd. We don't do a thing for two weeks. You get a bag of corn and put it in the garbage can left in the back of my office, and we'll take it up to Granny's barn. Both of the boys will be at work, and we can swap it out. I'll come up with a story about the corn and a trick on Hawthorn, but by then, he'll be in trouble. Well, he's already in trouble, but let's just say he will be found out by then, and we'll tell the boys we aren't going to trick him and play games because we don't like him anymore.

"The guys already know about Tammy, and soon, everybody will know about her and her lover, the ex-president of the Bank of Springo," Moon concluded his lecture.

"Well, they may keep it quiet about him and Tammy; just be in trouble because he left every Thursday," Lloyd stated.

"Listen, all a couple guys would have to do is to

tell Granny, Mattie Brown, Betty Smith, and Helen Schromisher."

"All you say is 'I heard...' and tell what we know about Thursdays, but always end it with, 'I don't believe it is so, just a rumor.' They'll argue with you that it is so, oh yes, *that woman.* They've heard how she acts at Moon Milligan's wild parties."

As the gangsters watched the rain fall on the soggy town of Springo, Lloyd exclaimed, "Moon, there's three deputy cars and two unmarked cars leaving the bank! They're heading over here, Moon! They're crossing the tracks."

"Hush, Lloyd. What do you think they did; take our picture with a garbage can? Calm down!" As the motorcade turned south, "Hello, Ms. Tammy and Mr. Bob, company's on the way." Moon, smiling in relief, burst into song.

"How did they figure it out this quick, Moon?"

"Well now, old friend, a little birdie chirped into Ms. Becky's ear about a banker not being where he told his secretary he was spending his time. You know, women don't like being lied to or like a man cheating on his wife. That Becky's a fine lady, honest as the day is long. Hello, Bob, we're on our way, and the sheriff is familiar with the path all the way to the bedroom. Oh, what a web they've woven."

Lloyd chuckled and said, "Moon, I'll never doubt anything you say again. But I have a question, has anyone outside the bank people ever seen one single dollar of money? Was the bank really robbed? *Ha, ha, ha.* Oh, me," he said as the gravedigger slapped his knees and laughed uncontrollably. "What kind of descriptions do they have about the robbers? Did one walk with a limp? One had a patch over his right eye, like a pirate, and they all got in a red Volkswagen, all six of them!"

"Stop!" Moon screamed as he laughed uncontrollably. As the friends enjoyed each other's company, not a single thought had gone to the burning question of any thief. *How much did we get?*

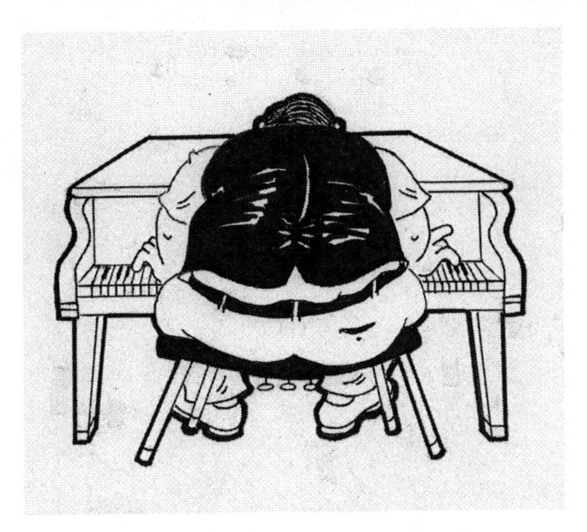

Investigation South

Suddenly, a county patrol car slid by the pumps and stopped in front of the door. An excited Deputy Morgan exploded, "It's Hawthorn. It's Hawthorn. He's dead!" he said.

"What do you mean?" Moon asked.

"He's dead. He had a heart attack at Johns,' the old retired banker . . . R.M. Johns III's house. They got the call, the TBI, sheriff, and everybody's headed that way. The bank robbers must have had him hostage down there."

"Bank robbers, what bank robbers?" Moon asked with a surprised expression.

"Oh, yea, cleaned out the bank over there," as the excited deputy pointed across the tracks.

Lloyd joined in. "When did it happen?"

"This morning. Think they locked that new boy, Jim Bates, in the vault. The state men were questioning him when I got there."

"How many robbers were there?" Moon asked.

"I don't know. They was on top of the Dime Store. Had scopes on their riffles. They were set to pick off any lawmen that might come in while they were robbing it. Their get away cars were over behind there! Had a man hiding by the railroad station. He had a machine gun or something big!"

"Which way did they go?" Lloyd questioned.

"Don't know. Had everybody lie down on the floor. Threatened to blow them away if they moved. Those poor women, you know the tellers, they were in shock, stuck guns in their mouths, said vulgar things to them. Boy, when we catch them, just let me at 'em," the spreader of truth said out of breath and finally silent.

As Deputy Morgan pulled away from the station, Lloyd turned to Moon.

"You know, I've known that guy for two or three years, ever since Sheriff McCoy got elected. I had no idea. That guy's a nut!"

"Well, he's off to the Johns' home. How much of his tale about Hawthorn dying down there is true?" Moon added.

As Stoker entered the Johns' home, he observed a covered body in front of the front door. He was met by Deputy Harwood. The coroner was sitting on the couch writing a report.

"Officer Harwood, Mr. Hawthorn, has he been positively identified as the dead man?" Stoker asked.

"Yes, sir. I personally know him," Harwood reported.

"How would that be, Officer?"

"I'm from Springo, and I bank at his bank."

"Who was here when you arrived, Officer?"

"Just Mrs. Johns and the deceased, sir. The coroner, Earl Thompson, over there on the couch, said it was a heart attack."

"There has been a bank robbery, and Mr. Hawthorn was the president of that bank. There was alleged information that he was being held hostage. Until we clear that up, we will secure this area," Stoker sternly ordered.

"I need to get Sheriff McCoy in here, sir. He's my commanding officer," Harwood bristled.

Sheriff McCoy and I have an understanding; he's to stay out of the crime scene if Mr. Hawthorn is a victim in any way. This house is a crime scene. Okay, Deputy?"

"Yes, sir."

"Mr. Thompson?"

"Yes, that's me. I'm presently acting as the county's coroner. In real life, I own a septic tank installation and cleaning business down in Graysville."

"I understand you have decided Mr. Hawthorn died of an apparent heart attack?"

"Yes, without a doubt."

"What was the scene when you got to the house, Mr. Thompson? Who was here? Who called you? Where was the body?"

"Now, that deputy you were talking to, don't remember his name, from up in Springo, he's the one that called and requested I come out. The body hasn't been moved since I got here. You see, the front door was locked ... had to come around to the side like you. The deputy said he locked the front door after he came around to the side and came into this room. Said Hawthorn must have fell right at the door and he didn't want everyone opening that door into the body. Now, the woman that lives here, let's see. I've got it in my report ... hmmm ... oh, yea, Tammy Johns. Now, this is what she told me, and it all makes sense. The dead man, he came to see her husband, and she asked him to step inside out of the rain while she went to call her husband, and when she got back, he was laying on the floor, just like he is now. The way she described him, he had fallen out all at once, and being dead that quick, it had to be his heart," the septic coroner concluded.

"Well, thank you, Mr. Thompson. By the way, why are you way over here on the couch doing your report, with those big chairs on that side of the room? They're closer to the body."

"Well, I tell you. Don't see too good, and that little lamp right here is the only light on in the house. Been like this since I got here. It's so dark over by the body, I could hardly see a thing. It's real dark and rainy. Been that way all morning. Must of got three or four inches."

As the agent walked over toward the body, two deputies came in. The sheriff said, "We are to help you any way we can."

"I'll need one more man."

"Deputy Harwood will be in. He's talking to his wife. She's afraid the creek up at Springo is going to get out of its banks. Said he'd be right in."

"What's your name, Deputy?"

"Billy Kaylor, sir."

"All right, Officer Kaylor, do you know Mrs. Tammy Johns?"

"No, sir, haven't met her."

"Good! Go to the back of the house and bring her to the kitchen. She's not to talk to anyone, do you understand?"

"Yes, sir."

"What's your buddy's name, Kaylor?"

"Tom Burton. He's just been with us a couple of weeks." "That's fine. Officer Burton, I need to speak with you for a moment. Burton, I want you to make sure all the doors to this house are secure. This is a crime scene. You stand by the side door that you just came in, after you have secured the house. Let no one in, except Mr. Johns, the owner, come get me if he shows up."

Agent Stoker walked over to the front door and stood surveying the scene. Shortly afterward, Officer Harwood returned.

"Sorry, sir. Now, how can I help?" the young deputy asked.

"The problem is lack of light. Do you have anything to help get better light on the body? How about getting that lamp over there and plugging it in over here? Hey, I'll let you handle the light problem. I want to have a word with Mrs. Johns."

Agent Stoker walked into the kitchen where Mrs. Johns was talking a mile a minute. Deputy Kaylor was standing without expression, listening.

"Oh, hi. I'm Tammy. How long before you can get him out of the house? My husband will be home soon."

"When you talked to your husband, did he say when he would be home?"

"Oh, I didn't talk to him. I knew he would be busy."

"Tell me from the start what happened here today, please?" Agent Stoker requested.

"Well, Bob ... I mean Mr. Hawthorn, came by to see my husband."

"What time was this?"

Looking quickly at her watch, she said, "It's after two now, so I would say about twelve, yes ... twelve."

"Step-by-step, go ahead."

"He came to the front door and rang the doorbell. I could barely hear it because it was raining cats and dogs." She giggled. "I opened the door, and he looked like a drowned rat. So I told him to step in out of the rain and I would call Mr. Johns to tell him he had company here at the house. I think they got their plans mixed up, you know, they're both getting kind of old. Well, I heard a thump as I was pouring a cup of coffee for Mr. Hawthorn, he was soaked, and his head was drenched. Didn't have an umbrella, hat, or anything. You know how you men are, think you are so tough. Well, I went back in the living room, and there he lay, dead as a mackerel. That's about it."

"Mrs. Johns, his car is parked under the carport. You have a wrap around porch ... how did he get so wet? Ah, never mind, continue," Agent Stoker stated as he deeply exhaled in disbelief.

"I called the sheriff, and they sent a deputy out, a sweet, young boy, Harwood I think, and he called the coroner. When they going to take him away?"

"Soon, Mrs. Johns. I'll be back in a minute."

As Agent Stoker walked into the front room, Harwood had it as bright as a TV studio.

"Where did you get all the lights, Deputy?"

"Here and there. Think that will be enough?"

"Looks good... ah... Mr. Thompson, what was the time of death?"

"Let's see. I got here about... ah... let me look at my report. Can't 'member squat. Looks like I got here at one ten, and the time of death was, let's see, left it blank. I believe Mrs. Johns said he dropped dead at twelve noon," the coroner reported. "I guess that's what I'll use... twelve."

"Deputy Harwood, when did you get the call?"

"Let me check, 11:21, sir. I wrote 11:21 in my log."

"What was the condition of the body when you arrived, Deputy, and the time?"

"Stiff as a board, Agent Stoker, and it was... ah... let's see, 11:39, sir."

"Was it raining when you got here?"

"Yes, sir."

"Was the clothing wet; his hair, shoes, anything?"

"No, come to think of it, he had a real clean, powdered smell!"

Agent Stoker took out an expandable pointer, leaned down, and lifted one of the deceased's pants legs, then the other. He stopped.

"Deputy, do you ever wear only one sock on a wet, January day?"

"No, sir."

"Help me take his pants down and his shirt off."

The pair pulled and tugged to get the banker's pants pulled down enough to see that his boxers were on backward. He couldn't get his arms uncrossed, but the agent had seen enough.

"Mr. Thompson, sign your report and let me have it. You can go on home. Thank you."

"You don't think it was a heart attack, do you?" Coroner Thompson asked.

"Oh, yes, I believe it was. Didn't happen at the time or place you've been told. Thank you, Mr. Thompson. Let yourself out."

"Harwood, ask the sheriff to come in here, please. He needs to make an arrest."

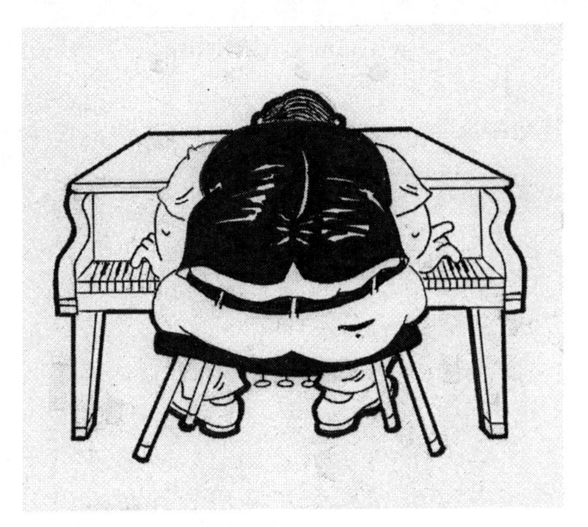

Gossip Headquarters

The word was spreading around Springo quicker than a cur puppy could lap up spilled milk. It was raining steady for at least the fifth day in a row. Either people were getting used to the weather or maybe they just wanted to get out of the house. Whatever the reason, Front Street was a popular venue as they splashed about; something to tell their grandchildren, how they had actually viewed the freshly robbed bank. It must be special. This was the same day the gang had invaded this wonderfully unspecial little town. "Oh yes, little Susie or little Johnny, your Granny saw the actual closed sign on the Bank of Springo."

The town's only dentist, Dr. Leonard, dropped by. Doc, as Moon called him, didn't beat around the bush.

"Moon, they beat us to it. Thought we could pull it off. Lloyd, you, and me, and get Jimmy Harrison to drive the get away car! They'll be watching everything now. We'll have to wait a while."

Moon replied without missing a beat, "Meigs County.

That's our target. All we have to do is see what these robbers do to get caught. Then we don't do that!"

"What about it, Lloyd?" the doc asked.

"Humph, leave me out. I won't be a part of no bank job."

The group sat talking about the events of the day. Doc said from what he had heard it seemed strange. There had been no description of robber or getaway car.

"You would think they would be putting out APBs. Oh, that's law talk for the description of suspects and the direction they are believed to be following," said Doc. "But what bothers me, I haven't seen the first cat or dog today!"

"What are you talking about, Doc?" a puzzled Moon asked.

"Several people have told me it was raining cats and dogs," he joked.

The response was silence.

"Oh no!" Lloyd exclaimed as a county patrol car turned into the station. "It's lying Morgan with the latest."

"No, that's the Harwood boy," Moon answered.

"Didn't know he was a deputy, and who's the fellow following him in that other car?" a puzzled Lloyd asked.

"It's a state man wearing a suit and driving an unmarked car," Moon stated as he began to feel flush with sweat droplets forming on his forehead.

"What do they want?" Lloyd asked to no one in particular but just searching for a calming response.

"They've come to investigate the robbery. Now here's what they're goin' to ask: did we see the direction of the robbers get a way?" Doc said as he started laughing and was halfheartedly joined by the nervous pair.

"Hi, fellows, most of you know me. I'm Tom Harwood with the sheriff's office, and this is Agent Stoker with the TBI. He's the lead investigator on the Springo Bank robbery."

"Agent Stoker, Moon Milligan, the station owner; Lloyd White, works for the funeral home here; and let's see, town dentist... I'm sorry, everyone just calls him Doc," an embarrassed deputy sputtered.

"Leonard, but Doc will be fine. Glad to meet you Agent Stoker. They went that a way," pointing north and drawing laughter.

"Best lead I've gotten today," the agent joined in.

"Mr. Milligan, is there somewhere we could talk?"

"I have an office in the back off the lube bay. Let me go clean it out so we can get in the door."

"Oh, don't worry doing that. It will be fine, I'm sure."

"No, we literally can't get in the room," Moon said, standing firm.

"Oh, okay, no problem," the agent answered.

Moon hastily exited the front and went to the rear of the bay. As he opened the door, he grabbed the two rescue squad radios laying on the littered desk and placed them in the trashcan and covered them with newspaper and ol' rags. Opening the door, he called for the agent and led him into the office.

"Mr. Milligan, I understand that Mr. Robert Hawthorn stops by here on Thursday mornings and purchases gasoline?"

"Yes, pretty much every Thursday."

"Did he stop by this morning?"

"Yes, he did."

"Do you remember what time it was and anything he had to say?"

Moon replied, "It was nine to nine thirty. I was busy inside and didn't wait on him. Hubert Lawson, he's mounting tires over in the next bay, he pumped his gas."

"How often did Mr. Hawthorn stop by?"

"Just about every Thursday morning. Always around the same time, has a bank meeting in Dayton, you know. It's amazing how punctual he is. I guess that goes with the territory of being a banker."

"Would you consider him a personal friend or just a customer, and oh, do you bank at his bank?"

"Let's stop right here, and let me ask you a question," Moon stated firmly.

"Go ahead, ask," Agent Stoker.

"Rumors are flying around like wild fire, small town, you know. We were told earlier today that Hawthorn was dead, had a heart attack, is that true?" Moon enquired. "And was it down at the Johns' home?"

"Yes, it was at the Johns' home. Because his bank was robbed, we will wait on a medical autopsy to determine if it was a heart attack, as it appears," the agent answered straight forwardly. "Mr. Milligan, now let's go back to my question about the extent of your relationship with Mr. Hawthorn."

"Hawthorn and his wife, Susanne, have attended parties that my wife and I have hosted at our home. Betty Jo, my wife, and Susanne Hawthorn are friends. Mrs. Hawthorn has shared some of her problems. I have been told that Mr. Hawthorn and Tammy Johns have been carrying on an affair for some time. I have lost any respect for the man. Mrs. Hawthorn is a sweet lady and has been a good friend. That Mrs. Thompson, she's a sweet lady and has always been extremely professional. Springo Bank is lucky to have her during this time of adjustment. By the way, I've heard all kinds of rumors about the bank. How many robbers and what were they driving, that's at the top of my curiosity," Moon inquired.

"I cannot comment on the bank robbery at this time. There's still a lot of investigating left to do. Mr. Milligan, please do not speak of anything we discussed except the death of Mr. Hawthorn. That's already public knowledge. I'm going to visit Mrs. Hawthorn, but I don't think she has any information that will help in this matter. Just have to dot my Is, you understand."

As the men walked back into the station front, Hubert and Lesiel had joined the great bank robbery discussion.

Lesiel asked, "Hey, are you the law?"

"I'm with the TBI," Agent Stoker answered with a nudge to Moon's arm as he walked up to the group.

"Well, what's that?"

"Tennessee Bureau of Investigation."

"Well, why don't you have no uniform on anyhow?"

"So the bank robbers won't know who I am."

"You got radar in your car out there?"

"No, I just catch bank robbers," the amused agent answered.

"Well, why ain't you caught 'em yet? Maybe cause you're in here a checkin' on Moon. He ain't robbed no bank. He ain't been out today; 'fraid he'd melt... ha, ha, ha, that a gooden, ain't it?"

Everyone laughed, ol' Lesiel sure did put that lawman in his place . . . yes siree!

Everyone seemed to enjoy the intellectual stimulation provided by Lesiel, except Deputy Harwood. He was embarrassed, as he had tried to be professional in front of Agent Stoker.

Moon thought as the officers left, *I'll bet Stoker would be a lot of fun off duty. Need to invite him to my next party.*

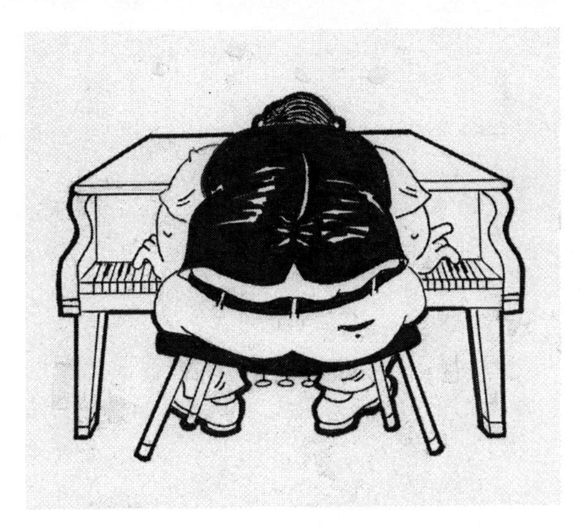

Bad News

A roll of thunder turned the remaining men's heads to the pouring rain just as the phone rang. Betty Jo's voice jump-started the big man's brain. He had not talked with her all day. There was so much to let her in on. Her best friend's husband was dead, the bank had been robbed ... her shaky, sobbing voice brought him back to the moment. *Someone's told her of Hawthorn's fate,* he thought.

"Moon, you've got to come home; it's Daddy. We've got to go. They've taken him to Athens Hospital; it's bad ... heart attack ... stroke ... please hurry!"

"I'm on my way. Lloyd, get Carl up here to take over and close up. It's Betty Jo's daddy. Got to go," Moon said as he ran to his car. Everyone was silent. The quick turn of events left everyone stunned. This day had been mind boggling; too much to absorb for the normally slow paced characters.

Heading out New Lake Road, Moon thought, *One*

thing had been constant all day, rain… depressing rain. When would he see the sunshine again?

As he entered the house, Jo came running from their bedroom. "Hold me; hold me." It was an unnecessary request, as the big guy already was pulling her close, as if trying to smother her sobs.

"Honey, I need to change my clothes."

"I have your clothes laid out. Please hurry!"

"I will, but come in the bedroom while I wash and dress. I don't want to take time to shower. Haven't been out of the office all day, anyway. There's something I need to tell you."

This was a bad time, but she needed to know about Susanne's husband. As he finished dressing and quickly gathered his billfold and keys, he walked into the kitchen. He heard Jo say, "I'm so sorry, Susanne. I wish I could be with you, but I must go."

She put the phone down, turned to him, and said, "Thank you for telling me about Bob. I don't know what I would do without *you.* Let's go!"

The trip, a normal thirty-minute drive, was much quicker. Moon, after all, had a heavy foot, and underneath the carpet was metal. So you see, this is where the saying "put the pedal to the metal was coined." As they arrived at the small community hospital, a family friend of Betty Jo's met them.

"Betty Jo, I'm sorry. He didn't make it."

Mr. Griffin had passed away fifteen minutes before Betty Jo and Moon had arrived. She turned to Moon, and the big guy cradled her in his arms in a loving embrace.

Mr. Griffin had passed at the age of sixty-seven. He had farmed and worked at various manual labor jobs since the age of fourteen. He was a good provider for his family and an honest man.

On Friday morning, the rain had diminished but showers still continued. The family's concern was an age-old prayer, "Please, Lord, don't let it rain on the funeral."

Moon sat in the living room with Betty Jo as the family planned the service. A neighbor lady, helping prepare food in the kitchen, tapped Moon on the shoulder. You have a phone call in the kitchen.

"Moon, Lloyd here. Sorry about Betty Jo's daddy, just found out this morning. Been callin' your house since six this morning. We got problems."

"What's the problem?"

"Piney flooded last night about eight and washed Granny's barn slap away, gone, down the creek. Mattie Brown's house and barn, gone. She was in her house when the water hit and almost didn't make it out. She grabbed a tree. One of the Thurman boys carried her to the street on his back. She's going to stay with the ol' lady and me. She said she had money put back, all gone now. We are lucky; we just lost a garbage can. What time is the funeral?"

"Don't know yet," Moon answered.

Moon drove back to Springo on Saturday morning to gather clothes for himself and Jo. Carl, with help from Hubert and Lesiel, had been working at the station. Moon stopped by to pick up the week's receipts and went to the bank to make a payment and get change for the station. As he walked into the bank, he noticed that Mrs. Thompson was at her desk and Mr. Hawthorn's office was dark. As she saw Moon enter the bank, she stood and walked directly over to him.

"So sorry to hear of the passing of Mr. Griffin. It's devastating to lose your father; I've been there. I hurt for Betty Jo. I know it was a shock to all of the family. I understand he and one of his son's had been out cleaning culverts to keep the water from getting up over the road," she concluded.

"Yes, but they had finished and he had just been sitting around the house for several hours. Got up to look out at the weather and dropped dead, right there in the living room."

"Everything's been crazy around the bank. They wouldn't let us open until eleven today, and poor Susanne, they didn't release Mr. Hawthorn's body until this morning. The funeral will be Monday. Are you going to be there?"

"Not unless Betty Jo goes. I'm going to try to stop

by Susanne's in a little bit. Just a bad situation," Moon answered.

"Did you know about Mr. Hawthorn and R.M. Johns' wife? I guess it's all over town by now. I've never been as shocked to find out about anything as this, and to think, I was covering for him without really knowing anything. Poor Susanne."

"Only knew what I was told secondhand!" Moon truthfully stated.

Before leaving Springo for his trip back to Meigs, he went by to see Susanne. As the visiting ladies left, she exchanged condolences with Moon and firmly stated, "You and Betty Jo are the only ones that have any knowledge that Bob had told me about not loving me. It would be easier to handle if I didn't have to hear about that in addition to his death. I still loved him. I want that to be my memory."

"Betty Jo and I will do anything we can to help you through this."

Susanne sobbed, "I couldn't have made it through this far without Jo."

As he crossed the tracks, Moon saw Lloyd's truck in its usual parking place. As he pulled up, he noticed a shiny, blue, late model Cadillac on the rack. Lesiel was placing a new tire on the left rear and Hubert was mounting another. Moon parked and walked over to Hubert.

"Hey, Moon, Mr. Johns came by to see you. Didn't know about Miss Betty Jo's daddy, said to pass on his ... ah ... conduits. We shure been a workin.'"

"That's good, Hubert. By the way, how did Mr. Johns know I'd have the tires to fit the caddy?"

"That Carl, he was, ah gasin' him up and he noticed

the front tars was a wearin' real bad on the one side and ah... Mr. Johns said he didn't have but about 18,000 miles on them. Carl said he needed to get out and look at em ... an ... da ... he did. Said didn't have time to get 'em lined up ... ah ... you know, Moon, kinda squared up sos they runnin' straight? Said if you got some new 'en to fit, we could put 'em on. We did, and we're a putt 'em on."

"Where is Mr. Johns now, Hubert?" a bewildered big guy asked.

"He called a lawyer guy from Dayton to come get him. Said he was a going to meet this here lawyer guy anyhow, and he did!"

As Moon stepped in the front, Lloyd said, "Carl had to leave for an hour or so. I came by to take his place. It's been real busy. Oh, Carl said Mr. Johns said to give his condolences to Betty Jo from him. Said just straight out with everyone standing in here that he kicked Tammy out."

"Well, what do you know? I'm surprised in a way, and then again, I bet this isn't the first time," Moon commented with a smile.

"Moon, while we're alone, let me give you an update. Two of Jim Boles's boys been going down the creek bank lookin' for stuff from the flood. I told you Mattie Brown was at our house, didn't I?"

"Yes."

"Well, those Boles's boys came over there this morning and handed Mattie $140, said they found it down the creek from her place. Jim told 'em that was the right thing to do. When they left, Mattie said the money wasn't hers because she didn't have any hundreds, and the hundred and the twenties were like new. She said she didn't say anything because the Lord had told her he would meet her needs, not to fear the water. She said he probably took it from a gambler or somebody that stole it. The Lord works in mysterious ways!"

"Moon," Lloyd continued, "Do you think I should tell those boys we had a big garbage can full of corn? If they find it with the lid on it, not to open it? The corn will suck up the dampness in the air and spoil?"

"We do not have a can missing, Lloyd! Forget about the money, it's gone. If you're not careful, Agent Stoker will be paying us a visit," Moon angrily stated.

"Okay, okay. You're right, Moon. Sorry."

"Don't worry about it, Lloyd. Ol' Hawthorn got the big lay off slip from the sky."

As he traveled back to Meigs County, Moon's mind began to wonder about Lesiel and Hubert. Not about anything they had said, but what they had not said. No questions about the bank robbery. Nothing said about the barn and its contents being washed away. Not even the missing garbage can and its effect on the *trick!*

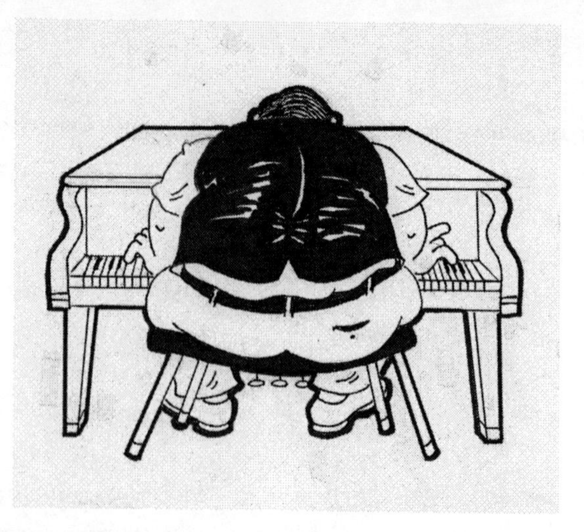

No Money, No Loss ... Maybe

Betty Jo held up as best as Moon could hope. After a couple hours at the family home, she was ready to return to Springo.

She was brought up-to-date on everything that Moon had knowledge of; everything except the participation by her husband and friends in the real robbery.

Her thoughts moved from her own sorrow to that of her friend, Susanne.

"Moon, could we just go straight up to Sue's house and see if there is anything we can do for her before tomorrow's funeral?" she asked.

"If you feel up to it, dear."

As they pulled into the Hawthorn driveway, Moon was shocked to see a shiny, light blue Cadillac. What would Mr. Johns be doing here at a time like this? He said nothing to Betty Jo.

As the couple entered the home, Mr. Johns was sitting at one end of the table and next to him sat a man

Moon had never seen before. A cup of coffee sat at the opposite end.

Susanne introduced Mr. Johns and the other gentleman, Roger Stonemoore. Though her eyes were red and swollen, she seemed in complete control of her emotions. Mr. Johns quickly stood and told Betty Jo of his sorrow for her loss. He then apologized for being there at a time like this, but as he had told Susanne, they had a mess on their hands.

He explained, "Sheriff McCoy has arrested Tammy at the urging of the TBI agent. The charge will not stick, something about altering a crime scene. She has requested a lawyer from Atlanta that she had used several years back. He had gotten her off on some drug charges and other problems that we won't go into. His name is Randy Nemire. Anyway, she still had her checkbook and wrote him a check for $5,000 as a retainer. I've closed that account but have to honor that check."

Mr. Stonemoore advised at this point that that would be the least of their worries. "It seems Mr. Hawthorn had written Tammy a promissory note for 50 percent of his estate if anything ever happened to him. Nemire has frozen all of the Hawthorn assets."

"Mr. Stonemoore has agreed to represent Mrs. Hawthorn as well as myself. He has been in contact with TBI Agent Stoker, and Stoker has agreed to help us any way he can. He thinks Tammy knows something about the bank robbery.

"I know Tammy, she's not that smart, and she can't keep a secret. But if Stoker makes her sweat, she will say or do anything to get out of this mess." Mr. Johns stated.

"Mrs. Hawthorn, I'm going to set up a checking

account in your name. I think that would be poetic justice. If you run low, let me know. I have money. How do you think I kept Tammy around?"

"By the way, Tammy signed a prenuptial agreement, but she has no idea what that means. When Nemire figures that out, and believe you me, he's strictly a drug lawyer in Atlanta, and this isn't Atlanta, Mr. Nemire will head south on 75 before you can say, 'See ya, Tammy,'" Mr. Johns chuckled.

"I'm leaving now, Mrs. Hawthorn, and I think it best I not attend the funeral. I don't want to be a distraction. I just can't imagine how hard this is on you. If I or Mr. Stonemoore can help, please call either of us any time, day or night."

"Mrs. Hawthorn, don't speak to anyone about the legal matters we have discussed here today, but make me aware of anyone from the other side trying to contact you," Lawyer Stonemoore explained.

As the lawyer and Mr. Johns were leaving, Becky Thompson and her husband, George, arrived. Moon and Betty Jo excused themselves, as Jo was tired and wanted to get home.

Sunday morning, Betty Jo was up early. The sun was showing its brilliance over the treetops of the nearby ridge. With the clearing came the cooling temperatures. The daily deluge of storms had brought uncharacteristic sixty-degree readings in January.

Betty woke the big guy and asked if they could go

to church. It had been a while since they had been there together. He was agreeable but negotiated for a breakfast of pancakes, sausage, bacon, and six eggs. Moon had an appetite.

"Want some of these eggs?" he asked, knowing she would turn them down.

"You know I wouldn't eat an egg if my life depended on it!"

The couple shared few common likes, but they had a deep, unbreakable love. Moon often said, "I'm the luckiest man in the world," and in the next breath, "She's driving me crazy, I need to get away... like ten years!"

After breakfast, the couple quickly dressed for church. "Come on, Moon, I don't like to walk in after church has started, you know everyone's eyes are on you, and I can feel my face getting red."

Moon grabbed Jo, pulling her close, kissing her long with passion.

"What was that for?" she asked.

"I just got back. I've been gone ten years," he answered as he exited the door.

"Men. Go figure," She thought as a smile curled from the corner of her mouth.

As the couple entered the church, they were pleasantly surprised to see Granny with Hubert. Moon and Jo sat across the aisle from the pair. After a few songs and the pastor's welcome, there was a greeting time. They stepped over to speak to Hubert and Granny, and a lady at the end of the pew greeted them.

"Hi, my name is Marie Traxwell, and this is my husband, Wesley, and these are our new friends, Hubert Lawson and his grandmother."

"Granny," Moon answered, "And she's a Lawson also," Moon quickly informed.

Where do these people come from? These new people come to town and treat us like we're not from around here, he thought but did not say.

Betty Jo, as so many times before, came to the rescue.

"I'm Betty Jo Milligan, and this is my husband, Moon, we own the Shell station here."

"Oh, I didn't know that. This is my husband, Wesley. Wesley, we will have to start trading with . . . ah . . . Mr. Moon."

Suddenly, this lady was talking his language, a customer. He could always use more customers.

"Hey, Wesley, bring 'er in for a free wash job when it warms up a bit. Oh, I'm talking about the car, not the wife."

Wesley's eyes dropped to the floor, and Marie turned away.

"Moon! I'll give you a call, Mrs. Traxwell."

As they returned to their seat, Betty Jo put her hand on the big guy's leg and her fingernails dug in.

"Ow," Moon responded. "Can't anyone take a joke?"

After church, Moon and Jo took Granny and Hubert to Mrs. Mathis's Restaurant for lunch. Granny related to them of her improving health. Her main topic of conversation was Lesiel. She said he was staying at home every night and didn't do anything but work. Guessed he had something on his mind. As they finished, Moon looked at his watch and commented, "I hate to go to funerals, but Jo, we better go on down to the Methodist church and pay our respects."

"It's for Susanne," she responded.

"I know," the big guy answered.

The Methodist church was packed as the Milligans entered. Moon took inventory—every politician in the county, bankers, and just about every businessman that had plied their wares in good ol' Springo or Rhea County, and Hawthorn's brother from Rossville, Georgia, he looked very much like his older brother.

Susanne had told Betty Jo that the brothers had a falling out over their father's will. It seemed he had favored young Randolph in the distribution of his assets. That's when Bob had left the bank his father had inherited from Bob's grandfather. Seemed like the whole bunch had more than their share of money issues.

The Milligans sat behind the Hawthorn family, and Moon noticed that Bob's loyal secretary, Becky Thompson, was the only one comforting Susanne. The rest of the family sat stoically by. Becky caught a glimpse of Betty Jo and motioned for her to move next to them. She shook her head in a negative response. Susanne turned and motioned for her, and Betty Jo responded.

As they were leaving the church, Moon noticed Lloyd slipping into his truck. It was parked at the distant corner of Church Street. Ol' Lloyd *does* have a heart. The gravedigger always said, "Shoot, I can talk to them when they get down to my place. Can tell 'em anything I want. They hardly ever talk back."

Lloyd, like himself, hadn't come to pay his respects to Hawthorn but to a sweet lady. Bet ol' Bob would sure get an earful if he hadn't boarded the elevator and watched as the down button was pushed.

As Betty Jo and Moon walked toward the gravesite, out of nowhere, a thought hit Moon. He couldn't contain it. He could just see Lloyd zipping around the graves as he mowed. Lloyd would stop, look all around, and then relieve himself on Hawthorn's grave. The Moon couldn't contain the images in his mind. He burst out laughing. Betty Jo poked him in the ribs, but he couldn't stop. It was a time of healing.

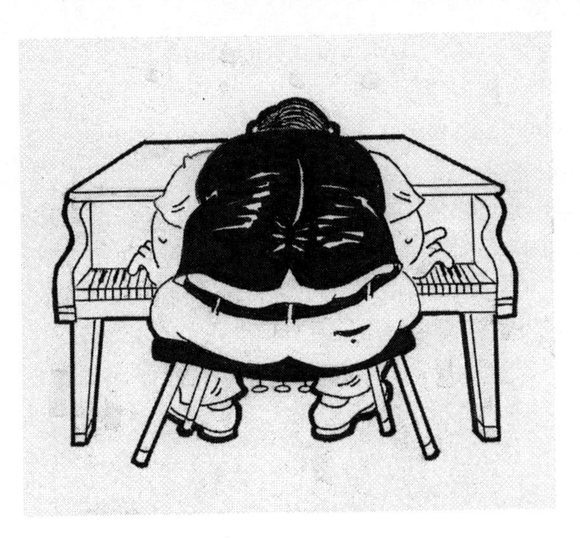

A New Party

The days of spring came and were slowly slipping into summer. Moon had made a big decision. He was going to have a party at his house. A party like never before. A party so tame Granny would be a special guest, God bless her and may her soul rest in peace ... ah, when her time came, of course.

Springo had been a feature story of Channel Nine News from Chattanooga. It was about a little, sleepy town that had an unsolved bank robbery. The news crew spent several days interviewing residents, but of course, they had to find the most eccentric ones, like Marlin Bright. His story quickly turned to the Hawaiian Islands and his memories of working there during and after WWII. Anchor Mort Floyd seemed to delight in this. They did, however, have a very good interview with Becky Thompson, the acting bank manager. They used words such as *unusual circumstances* of Hawthorn's death. They were unable to get any new information from the sheriff's office or TBI.

The amount taken was always referred to as *undetermined.*

"Hey, come on, the people want to know," Moon would say each time the bank job was brought up.

The truth is, Moon was really curious; he told Lloyd he just couldn't get that question out of his head.

The most unusual change was Mr. Johns. R.M. had become a regular at the station. In fact, he spent a lot of time in Springo. He enjoyed listening to Hubert and Lesiel. Lesiel was a little uneasy around Miss Tammy's ex-main man. He and Hubert were often asked to tell about the deer that came alive. R.M. and his lawyer friend, Roger Stonemoore, who often accompanied the retired banker to Springo, laughed until tears came to their eyes.

Hubert and Lesiel had very little small talk with Moon; Lesiel, in particular, had little to say.

Betty Jo was excited about the party, mostly because of the absence of alcohol. She wasn't a prude, but the friends she wanted to invite wouldn't come if there was alcohol, or if they did, they would have to leave early and most would politely make excuses if invited again.

Moon drank much less than most thought. He would start off all the events with Coca-Cola on the rocks. Jo would always prepare his drinks as he preformed. Many nights, he never asked for a Coke, his code for a mixed drink. For the first time in many years, Betty Jo made a list of potential attendees. At the top of her list were her two youngest sisters and her brother, Tom. Tom had been preaching since the first of the year.

Susanne quickly accepted an invitation and giggled about bringing a special guest. The unnamed guest was no mystery to Betty Jo and Moon.

Will Norris and Mabel were coming. It had been over six months since Will had taken a drink. He was constantly getting on Moon about attending church more often.

George and Becky Thompson were coming, and for a first-ever appearance would be Moon's best friend, Lloyd White, the gravedigger. His schedule was open that particular Friday night.

Preacher Booker had a previous engagement, but Deputy Harwood said he was thankful for the invitation. The rumor around town was that he would be running for sheriff in the upcoming election.

Agent Robert Stoker said if he could clear the evening from a training session, he and his wife would be there. He said his wife, Judy, would be looking forward to seeing some of the characters she had heard about. Robert explained she was from a small, south Georgia town of twelve hundred and missed the people and friendly neighbors. He sure liked Springo and wanted to show her the area.

Forrest Robbins, brother of Pig, was coming. He was an accomplished musician in his own right.

The day of the event had arrived, and Betty Jo sensed something she never observed coming from her husband. He seemed nervous ... concerned about arrangements for the evening, as if they hadn't partied before.

"Do we have enough soft drinks ... you know, that's all the drinks we'll have?"

"Yes, dear, I've got enough."

"What about food? We're going to start the grill, aren't we?"

"Yes, dear. I've bought enough of everything."

"What are we going to do when I'm not playing? You know, I'm used to playing from start until no one's left standing."

"Moon! Stop it. We'll talk to our guests, not about them! It will be all right, and it will be over at a reasonable hour, no 2:00 a.m. parties ever again."

"Never?" he asked.

"Never. Now just go to work!"

As Moon walked out the door, he said, "I'm so glad none of my buddies were here, witnessing her talk to me like this. Sometimes I just *think* I'm the boss . . . I think," he admitted to his dog, Floppy, and himself.

Moon entered his work domain with renewed energy and self-confidence. Business had been really good. He unlocked the front door and moved to the cash register to put the start-up money in.

"I'm the boss. Hey, I'm the Boss Hog. Tee hee."

"What are you talking about? And who are you talking too?"

A startled station owner with cash in hand turned around

to a smiling gravedigger.

"It's a good thing I don't have my .38 in my pocket."

"It would take you thirty minutes to get it out, and I would be long gone," the friend teased.

Moon asked, "Lloyd, all joking aside, could you come a little early tonight and help me set up?"

"Don't know if I can get out of the house. That woman doesn't like me leaving after dark."

"That woman's got a name, you old coot. It's time you started giving her some respect. Now, Gracie will come. Jo's already talked to her. You tell her we're expecting both of you, understand!"

Moon talked with the boys when they got to work. Hubert said he was bringing Granny, and she had fixed a big batch of fudge.

"She wouldn't let us have nary a piece," he stated.

Lesiel kept quiet, as had become his standard reaction to most all the goings on at the station.

"Lesiel," Moon raised his voice, "I need your help, and I expect you to be there, do you understand?"

"Yea, I'll be there."

Wesley Traxwell stopped, filled up, and pulled to the side of the station, and then got out to wait. Moon was busy with another customer. As he finished, Wesley walked up and as if giving the big guy a direct quote, "We're looking forward to the event at Mrs. Milligan's and your home. What should myself and Mrs. Traxwell bring?"

"Just come enjoy yourselves, and loosen up, man. We're just average folks getting by with a below average IQ."

"We'll be there at 7:00 p.m., looking forward to the event," a stoic Traxwell responded.

As he returned to his car, Moon thought, *This town needs to start a right to life chapter for this guy.*

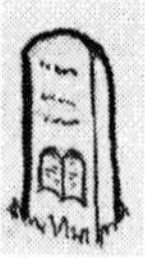

Granny, Lesiel, and Hubert were the first to arrive. Lloyd and that woman, Gracie, came shortly afterwards. Lesiel was eager to do his job starting the grill.

"Got any kerosene, Moon?" he asked.

"Use this lighter fluid," he said, handing a can of charcoal lighter fluid to the cook master.

"Lesiel, tell 'em about the time you got the kerosene can and it wasn't, it was the gas can," Hubert prodded.

"Wasn't no big deal, just went *whoosh* and singed my hair some."

"No big deal my foot, you didn't have no eyelids or eyebrows, and it made the top of the porch roof black, and what about Granny's morning glories at the end of the porch? Leaves dried up like December and a it was July!"

For the first time in months, Moon saw a sheepish grin come from Lesiel.

"Well, if the truth was known, ol' Hubert put gas in the kerosene can," Lloyd kiddingly added.

"No I didn't. No, no, no, sir, buddy! No way."

The three said in unison, "Yes you did, yes you did," pointing at Hubert.

It was a good start to the evening.

As a car drove slowly by the house and then backed up, Moon recognized Agent Stoker. He walked out toward the road and motioned them into the driveway. Brenda jumped out of the car.

"Well, hello! You must be Moon!"

"Now, how did you figure out it was me?" the big guy kidded.

"'Cause you're the biggest, and from what I've been told, the best piano player in the country and parts of Europe."

It was love at first sight for Moon.

"Before a lot of people get here, Brenda and I have a favor to ask, if you're not too busy tomorrow," Robert requested.

"I don't babysit," Moon stated before Robert could get his request out.

"Why, I'd trust Hubert and Lesiel with my kids before you, you old reprobate," he laughed and then continued. "Brenda and I are going to move away from Chattanooga, and I sure like Springo and the people I've met under difficult circumstances. We were wondering if Betty Jo and you would have time to show us the area tomorrow, if we drive up?"

"Sure, but I thought you had to be on call and close to the office down there?" Moon questioned.

"I'm changing jobs. Anyway, we'll tell you all about it tomorrow. Right now I'm going to take Brenda in to meet Betty Jo," the new friend stated firmly.

Moon's thoughts were: *I like that guy and his wife. Hope she hits it off with Jo.*

The crowd continued to grow, and Betty Jo said to Moon, "I think this is the largest group we've ever had in our house, and half of these people haven't heard you play. Would you come in and play a little dinner music while people start fixing their plates? Hey, you know the best thing?" she asked.

"What?"

"No one came just to get drunk or to try to hit on someone's wife."

"Well now, honey, I've already given Brenda Stoker my best shot."

"Dream on old man, she doesn't want you *now,* and when I get through with you, she's not going to volunteer to wheel you around while your broken legs heal!" she laughed.

As everyone settled in and began to eat, Moon slid his bench close to the piano and hit a few notes to tune up. He looked, and all eyes were on him. Betty Jo, for the first time, had joined his audience. She was sitting next to *that woman,* Gracie White.

Moon started playing a slow, mellow tune as everyone returned to eating and conversation. He couldn't help it, the mischief came out. *Bam,* everyone looked up as he started pounding out a Little Richard number. He had gotten the attention of the hostess, and just as quickly, he returned to his original selection. Jo continued to put the evil eye on him for several minutes. His smile and wink eventually won her over. Moon could smell the aroma from the grill wafting in from the patio. Hunger pains attacked him with a vengeance. He motioned for Forrest Robbins to play. Forrest, like his brother, Pig, was an accomplished musician. He played the guitar in several bands over the years, but it was rare for him to play solo.

As the big guy was stacking burgers on his plate like they were pancakes, he heard a strong, smooth voice coming from his living room.

"Man, that Forrest has a voice. I've never noticed it."

"Probably because you're too busy trying to figure out

the keys to your piano," Lloyd fired at him, joined by snickers from Hubert and Lesiel.

"Awww, you're unhappy because you're not out talking to the headstones, you ol' gravedigger!"

As the get together was winding down, Marie Traxwell stood and gently tapped her fork on her glass. "I would like to thank the Milligans for inviting us into their home, and most importantly, for making us feel at home in your Springo.

"Weather permitting, Wesley and I would like to host a picnic at the city park for everyone here. Especially bring your children, and let this be in honor of Betty Jo and Moon. I'll bet some of you are not aware of the new service Mr. Moon offers at his station. Wesley took me by there today, and I got a free wash job. Didn't need a bath before coming out tonight, isn't that right, Wesley? By the way, Mr. Moon, I might suggest you use softer brushes, the whitewall brush was a little coarse on my back."

The crowd howled with laughter, and Moon thought, *That ol' girl's all right, but someone needs to clue Wesley in.* The last of the guests had gone, and there were a bunch of minutes left before midnight.

"Moon, this is the first party we've hosted that the kitchen was cleaned up before everyone left, and Granny, bless her heart, said this was the first time in years she had been invited to someone's house. You could tell she had such a good time. She and Susanne talked the whole time. R.M. was talking with you men."

"Jo, come sit beside me and I'll play a love song and sing it just to you."

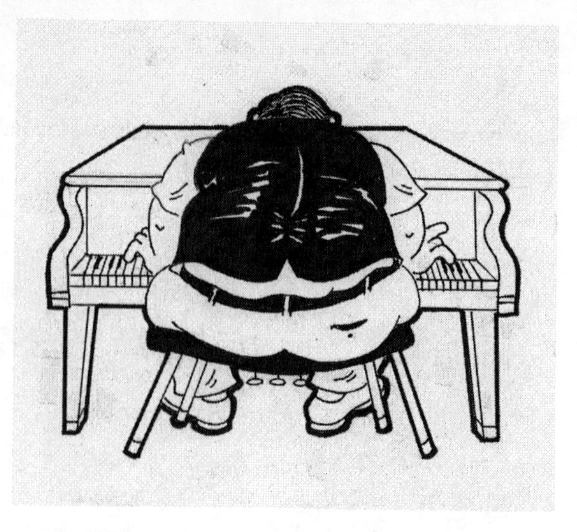

Answers, New Questions

Lloyd was waiting on Moon to arrive so he could get on with his Saturday. He was only scheduled to work Monday through Friday, but that had been altered through the years. He always showed up on Saturday and checked to see if there were any new plantings scheduled. After his visit to the funeral home, he would mosey (yes, in it's true meaning, to move in a leisurely or aimless manner) down to the cemetery and check first for vandalism and then pick up any trash from overnight lovers. If it was a time of rapid growth, he might mow for a few hours to keep from getting behind.

On the plus side of this unspoken, unwritten agreement, he visited around town, took care of his business, or on some days, just took a ride. This morning he planned to take extra time to get updated on Moon's goings on.

"Hey, Moon, what did Stoker have to say? Learn anything?"

"You were at the same party I attended, Lloyd."

"I heard something about you all getting together today," inquired a nosey gravedigger.

"He's thinking about moving up this way, Lloyd. Get over it. The bank job is a thing of the past. No money, no arrests," Moon concluded.

Hubert and Lesiel joined in on the conversation about the state of the world affairs. It was like the good ol' days... almost. Moon told the fellows that he had brought a sack full of leftovers from the party and placed the burgers in the cooler. He told them that if he was gone with the Stokers at lunchtime, to get it out and eat all they wanted. Carl was coming in at ten to help out.

Robert and Brenda Stoker pulled into the station, and Moon got in his Lincoln and the couple followed him out to his house to pick up Betty Jo. Robert said they would like to look at the area around the lake, but it didn't have to be right on the lake. Brenda said they would be moving soon and didn't have time to build.

Moon couldn't stand it any longer.

"What will you be doing, Robert?"

"I've taken a job with the state controllers office. I'll be in charge of East Tennessee from the Georgia border all the way to Bristol. It will include Chattanooga, Knoxville, and the tri-cities area and everything in between. I have to be in Nashville about ten days a month, except budget time, then I'll be there as long as a month. I won't be called out at night or have to work weekends if someone robs a bank."

"Well, I hope you do a better job controlling them than you do at catching bank robbers," Moon joked.

"My advice to you, Mr. Gas Man, is to get an extra tank buried at the station, cause this controller's going to be burning that Shell TCP."

"Hey, guys, let's find a place to live," Brenda ordered.

"Well, Miss Brenda, I'm taking you out to see the countryside around the Wolf Creek area of Watt's Bar Lake. After that, we'll stop at Pete Smith's Watt's Bar Resort for lunch, then at two, we are to meet Jack Phillips to look at some real estate listings ... so there!"

Everything went as planned, and the Stokers found several places of interest. Moon could tell that both had fallen in love with a newer home with four acres and about 1,000 feet of lake frontage with a nice dock. As always, the nicest thing you see comes with a budget-breaking price.

As they arrived back at the Milligans' home, Moon wanted to check on the station, so he and Robert went to town and left the women to their girl talk.

As soon as they left the house, Robert said, "Let's go somewhere so we can talk."

"Would you smoke a good cigar, Agent?"

"Hadn't had a cigar in ages. Sure, you got one?"

"I'll stop by the station. I've got a box of Cubans Pig Robbins gave me for Christmas. Got 'em hidden in the back room."

"No telling what you've got hid back there," Robert laughed.

Lloyd and Bear were in deep conversation as Moon and Robert pulled into the station.

"Well, the affairs of the world are in order with those two in charge," Moon laughed.

"This is what I enjoy about a small town," Robert commented.

"Hey, watch it. Springo's not all that small."

"Hey, Lloyd, any diggin' going on down at the cemetery today?"

"Nope, mighty quiet down there this time of day; everybody's resting up for their nightly activities."

"See you, fellows," Bear grunted as he walked out the door.

Moon retrieved the cigars and checked the register, turned to Carl, and said, "Be back to close. We're going to go down to the cemetery and smoke a cigar and figure out how to rob a bank."

As the Lincoln traveled down Cemetery Road, Robert was busting at the seams to start talking.

"Moon, I'm going to tell you something about the Springo Bank robbery that has some of the best robbery experts in the southeast stumped.

"I have a feeling, someday, someone will talk, and again, maybe not.

"This is the first robbery anyone has ever investigated where more money was taken than was supposed to be there."

"Robert, I've heard a hundred thousand dollars was taken; how much was it?" Moon enquired.

"The closest we can figure is between two hundred and two hundred fifty thousand dollars."

Moon's jaw dropped. "You've got to be kidding me!"

"The inventory records Mrs. Thompson had and the first set we found in Mr. Hawthorn's locked drawer matched and were right on the money down to the penny of what they should have had according to deposits, paid outs, and their financial dealings: $117, 314.

"Mrs. Thompson had a problem with that. As she was filling boxes according to the demands of the robbers, she was shocked to find $100 bundles stacked under bundles of ten-dollar bills. The hundreds weren't on the shelf where they should have been.

"She said she was nervous, and the amount could not be confirmed, due to the haste of the filling of the boxes, but she swore there was at least $175,000 in one-hundred dollar bundles.

"I interviewed the Bates young man separately, and he guessed there was $100,000 in hundred-dollar bundles. He filled the can to the brim, and there were additional boxes filled with money.

"Our lab in Knoxville got one of those large trash cans that Bates described from the factory in Athens and placed the correct amount of ones, fives, tens, twenties, and fifties that both inventory records showed. It filled the can almost to the top, very little room left for bundles of one-hundred dollar bills.

"When we found a third set of records tucked in a *Saturday Evening Post* in Mr. Hawthorn's unlocked, top drawer, we were dumbfounded.

"In chronological order, it listed deposits each Friday, starting about three months after Hawthorn started there. They varied from $2,000 up to $10,000.

"A complete in-depth check of the Hawthorns' financial records, savings, checking, and investments was done, and there were no conflicting figures. The last entry was made on the Friday before the robbery. There were no unaccountable withdrawals before the robbery."

"Do you think Hawthorn had anything to do with the robbery?" Moon asked.

"Yes, definitely, but we just can't tie anything together."

Moon questioned, "What about Tammy?"

"No, we interviewed her sober, and while she was under the influence of drugs at the Red Bank Police Department, she's not a very smart person, nor loyal. She would dump on anyone to get a break for herself.

"Moon, your name was on our list for a while."

"How in the world did you come up with that? I still don't get it. No one saw anything or anybody except for the person on the Five and Ten roof, from what I hear."

"It was the garbage cans you got from your neighbor at the Gulf Station. He was the only person in Springo to buy cans from the fellow from Athens. Did you know they were seconds?"

"Yes, I gave five dollars each for them. Why didn't you take me in for questioning?" Moon asked.

"Those cans were sold all the way from Knox County to Bradley and Hamilton County. Oh, yeah, the cans sold to Mr. Lyons were stolen. The seconds that the factory sold were eight dollars. You got a deal, Moon."

"Well, Robert, you tell me how this bank job went down."

"I think Hawthorn engineered the whole thing. He used Tammy to provide an alibi, if worse came to worse. After all, a divorce is better than prison," Robert continued.

"Tammy said when he got there that morning, he went into the bedroom, shut the door, and got on the phone, running her out of the room. We got the phone records; the calls were made to a phone booth. After that, he calls for Tammy, they have sex, and he rolled over, made a strange sound, and was dead. She admitted to dressing him and dragging him to the living room. She said she went into the kitchen, poured a cup of coffee, spiked it with Vodka, and tried to call the sheriff, but they wouldn't patch her in to him. She waited a while and called the sheriff's office and told them a man had dropped dead at her front door."

"Where's the money?" Moon asked.

"My guess would be three or four good ol' North Georgia boys have new four-wheeler trucks and new double wides with swimming pools," concluded the soon-to-be ex-Agent Stoker.

At the first opportunity, Moon relayed the information he had gleaned from Robert to Lloyd.

"You know, Moon, it doesn't cross my mind anymore. It's like we never took that money from the bank."

"Did you look inside the garbage can or open one of the boxes, Lloyd?" Moon asked.

"No."

"Well, think about it. No guns, never stepped foot in the bank, didn't see any money, that day or after, right?"

"Right, Moon!"

"Case closed. Back to the present. Marie Traxwell has invited all of us that attended the party last week to a family picnic down at Veteran's Park a week from Saturday," Moon reported.

"Oh, I know! *That woman* already told me we were going. Betty Jo and Mrs. Traxwell done called her. She said Mattie was invited too, and she's going to come with us."

Moon said, after a long pause, "I invited Mattie to the party at my house. Wonder why she didn't come then?"

"Oh, she had to keep our kids for us so we could come," Lloyd explained.

"You don't have any kids. Quit being so smart mouthed!" Moon raised his voice.

With a grin, "Maybe she didn't want to go to the home of the biggest, meanest, loudest, redneck in Springo, awww... did I say ugliest and hot tempered?" Lloyd blasted his friend as he slapped his knee in delight.

It had been on rare occasions that the gravedigger could get to the big guy, and he was enjoying every second. Moon saw the delight in Lloyd's face and decided to cut his losses.

"You think it might have been the George Wallace signs I've still got up in my yard?"

Times were good for the big guy. He had hired Carl fulltime, and Hubert and Lesiel were being paid wages also.

The next morning, Mr. Johns asked Moon if he had time to go for a ride with him. There were several regulars setting around arguing about the upcoming elections, and R.M. said he wanted Moon to look at some property with him. As the two men pulled away in the blue Caddy, the banker wasted little time getting to his purpose for the drive.

"Went to court yesterday, had a hearing about Tammy's claim to half of Hawthorn's estate. The judge ruled that the promissory note Hawthorn had written her for half of his estate was null and void. He ruled it was unwitnessed, undated, and made no reference to the legal will on record at the courthouse. Besides, due to the circumstances of the presentation, it was void because it was payment for sexual favors and prostitution is illegal in Tennessee. Her lawyer, Randy Nemire, was out of there before the echo of the judge's gavel had cleared. Couldn't help but feel sorry for Tammy. The judge ordered her back to jail until a public defender could prepare for the six or seven charges against her, ranging from drugs to bad checks and shop lifting."

"I thought it would be proper if you went with me to relay the good news to Susanne. Stonemoore is tied up in court today. I think the world of Susanne, but I think I need to bow out, because every time she sees me, it has to remind her of the terrible situation Bob got himself into and his ongoing involvement with Tammy.

"It's different with me. I married Tammy fully aware of her past. I mistakenly thought I could change her."

Moon sat silently for a moment, then said, "Don't just walk away cold turkey. She's been leaning on you since the day her husband died. She needs friends, and remember, she didn't enter into her marriage as you did yours." Moon continued, "Ask her if she wants to go to the picnic."

"Yes, thanks for the advice. I think the picnic would be good for both Susanne and me." R.M. smiled.

As Moon sat at Susanne's kitchen table, the three laughed and talked of the party and Hubert and Lesiel. Susanne thought they were charming. Moon, never in his life, would go there.

Betty Jo and Moon took their Jeep to the park for the picnic. They hàd eight watermelons that the big guy had purchased from a man gassing up at the station.

"Moon, did you see any of the watermelons cut that the guy had?" she asked.

"No."

"Don't you think you should plug one and make sure they are ripe?"

"No."

The crowd was larger than at the Milligans' party, as several guests brought extended family, and the fear of the wild drunken orgies at Moon's sponsored events had been dispelled by the gossip ladies. You see, Granny had been dispensed to Moon's party to get dirt on the big guy. Surprisingly, though, he come out clean, and Granny was lettin' everybody hear about it.

Lloyd, the gravedigger, was in charge of the grill crew. His able assistants were Hubert, Lesiel, and Doc. Doc was there to give a quick dental exam if anyone bit on anything hard.

Moon did not play, did not cook, and did not partake of any beverage that wouldn't have been found at a church social. He enjoyed the people and was totally relaxed.

It was a storybook day in every way, from the gently cooling breeze rustling through the treetops to the glistening ripple of the lake water just a stone's throw away. The squeak of swings signaled children at play. It was a perfect day.

Moon glanced up toward the parking area and recognized a man approaching. He was with a woman that Moon hadn't met.

"Jerry Underwood, who's the good looking woman you paid to run around with you?"

"This is my wife, Linda. We've been married four years,"

Jerry answered.

"Hi, Linda. I'm Moon. Jerry led the football team down the field in high school, and I tried to lead all the girls astray," the big man boasted as he glanced over his shoulder to see if Jo was listened.

"What brings you to Springo?" Moon asked.

"Had a little family business to take care of. We stopped by the station, and they told me you were down here. Been lookin' forward to finding out the latest on the bank heist," the ol' classmate stated.

"Well, I'd almost forgotten about Springo's day of fame. I wonder from time to time if there was really a robber or if the news folks made it all up."

"That's not what I hear from Tom Givens. He's my

next-door neighbor down in Hixson. Tom works with Agent Stoker of the TBI. Tom said it was an inside job with some local help. You, Moon... you're my guess. Had an eye on you since high school. I remember when you tried to set the band room on fire but Miss Glover caught you and kicked you out of chorus."

"You were the snitch! I knew somebody ratted me out. By the way, Jerry, Robert Stoker and his wife, Brenda, are standing over there talking to Betty Jo. Now what did this Givens guy have to say?" Moon inquired.

"He thinks the money was stashed inside the bank and then removed once the state had finished with their investigation. He said it could have been the banker that died and his secretary. He said they were real close," Jerry ended.

"He's so far out in left field, he can't see home plate. He probably thinks we'll put a man on the moon. Get real, Jerry. Let's go fix you and the little woman a burger."

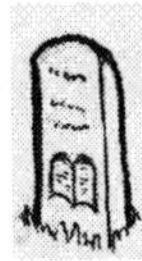

As the shade from giant poplar trees began to lean to the east, the cooks finished cleaning the grills. Lloyd walked over to Moon, Jo, and Gracie.

"Hey, ya'll! Want to walk over to Piney, and I'll show you where I learned to swim?"

The ladies looked at each other and answered in unison, "No, you guys go on."

Lloyd and Moon walked the fifty yards or so over to the creek, Lloyd talking all the way.

"You know, Gracie has been so happy ever since she

met some of the ladies out at your party. They talk on the phone, and she's not as worried about who I'm talking too. She doesn't stand by the door and want to hear why I'm ten minutes late getting home from the cemetery. She acts like she's twenty years younger. Oh, Moon, right down here, my oldest brother pitched me in and said, 'Swim boy,' and I sure—"

"Hey, Lloyd, what's that?" Moon almost screamed.

"What, Moon?"

"Look on that snag fluttering in the swift water. See it?"

"Yes! Yes!" in a barley audible voice. "Moon, it's money . . . a bill!"

Moon ordered, "Get a stick and fish it out!"

"Okay, here's one. Hold my belt so I can lean out to snag it. There, I got it. It's a one hundred dollar bill, Moon! Oh! It's gone . . . the current . . . ah."

Moon looked at Lloyd as their eyes met. Their faces drained into sullen expressions. They both turned in unison and stared into the depths of Piney River.